In the Wild

SOFIA NORDIN

In the Wild

TRANSLATED BY
MARIA LUNDIN

A GROUNDWOOD BOOK
HOUSE OF ANANSI PRESS
TORONTO BERKELEY

Copyright © 2003 by Sofia Nordin
Translation copyright © 2005 by Maria Lundin
First published in 2003 as *Aventyrsveckan*
by Eriksson & Lindgren Bokförlag AB, Stockholm, Sweden.
First English edition published in 2005.

Groundwood Books / House of Anansi Press
110 Spadina Avenue, Suite 801, Toronto, Ontario M5V 2K4

Distributed in the USA by Publishers Group West
1700 Fourth Street, Berkeley, CA 94710

Groundwood Books thanks the Swedish Institute
for its generous support of this translation.

Library and Archives Canada Cataloguing in Publication
Nordin, Sofia
In the wild / by Sofia Nordin;
translated by Maria Lundin.
Translation of: Aventyrsveckan.
ISBN 0-88899-648-9 (bound). — ISBN 0-88899-663-2 (pbk).
I. Lundin, Maria II. Title.
PZ7.N77In 2005   j839.73'8   C2004-906455-X

Cover illustration by Doug Martin
Design by Michael Solomon
Printed in Canada

In the Wild

Chapter One

WE'RE HEADING UP NORTH on an adventure trip. The school has rented a bus just for us and everybody is gathered in the schoolyard with their luggage, waiting for the bus to arrive. Philip and Andrew and a few other guys are running in circles around the whole class, chasing each other on the gravelly asphalt, shouting as they go. Teacher looks at them with a frustrated expression, and then smiles at the three parents who are there to chaperone. It's one of Teacher's special, meaningful smiles, like she's saying, "These kids are impossible, aren't they?"

Cecilia's mom is there, and Dunja's mom and Adam's dad. It's pretty obvious that Adam is embarrassed that his dad is coming on the trip with us. It's going to be hard for him to be his normal self when his dad is there watching all the time.

Vanya, Cecilia and Olivia are standing in a little group, whispering and giggling. They're sharing their make-up brushes and lipsticks and a new kind of mascara that's supposed to give them irresistibly long and thick eyelashes. Now and then they look up at the guys racing around and then look back at each other, rolling their eyes.

"God, they are *so* childish," sighs Vanya.

"Yeah, totally immature," say Cecilia and Olivia, copying the condescending look on Vanya's face.

I just stand there, moving a little pile of gravel back and forth with my left foot, trying to look like it's incredibly interesting to move pebbles around the schoolyard. That way it might not be so obvious that no one's talking to me. If I look occupied then maybe Teacher won't come up and put her arm around my shoulders and say, "Amanda, why are you standing here all alone?" She's done that a few times before, and the only thing more embarrassing than that is when she pulls me around the schoolyard "to find someone for you to play with." She's done it twice, and both times I was teased about it for weeks.

Suddenly, Philip leaps past and kicks my backpack. Before I have time to react, he's gone again. When he runs past again on his next loop around the playground, he hisses at me between his teeth so Teacher can't hear him.

"Hey, nice backpack! Where'd you find it, in the trash?"

Before I have a chance to answer, he's headed off again in the other direction. I stand there, staring at my backpack. I don't see what's wrong with it. It's not like it's dirty or ripped or anything. And besides, it's the exact same brand as several of the other bags that are sitting on the pavement waiting to be loaded onto the bus. Not the same brand that the coolest people in our class carry, of course, but not some horrible, outlawed brand either.

When the bus drives into the schoolyard we all cheer and whistle. It's green and white and a bit dusty, and the driver looks nice. She says a friendly hello and steps out to open up the luggage compartments.

When I go to toss my backpack into one of the compartments, Philip is suddenly right there next to me again.

"That's a really cool backpack, actually," he whispers with a sneer. "Too bad it smells so disgusting. I guess I'll have to put my bag somewhere else."

Even though I know that my bag doesn't smell like anything in particular, I can't help bending down and pretending to look for something in the front pocket, just so I can sniff it a little. My pack is definitely filled with smells, but they're faint, and besides, they're anything but disgusting. The camping mat that's strapped to the top has a nice woodsy smell, left over from the last time Mom and Dad and Sebastian and I went "adventuring" as we call it. And the pack itself has a faint smell of campfire — more like the memory of a smell.

As I board the bus, the first thing I do is look at the sign at the front that says how many seats there are.

Forty-five. Phew. Forty-five seats. More seats than

people. No one will have to sit next to me. I hate the look on my classmates' faces when they realize that the only seat left is next to me. It happens almost every day in the cafeteria, and when we take the bus or subway for field trips. Sometimes whoever is stuck without a seat will try to stand in the aisle instead, but our teacher always comes over and points out, "Look, there's a spot next to Amanda!"

Then when they actually sit down, they usually try to pretend that they're not sitting next to me at all, like I don't exist. You should see the weird positions they get into so that they don't have to look at me. Not everyone does that, of course. Some of them are nice. Emily is always pretty decent, and Adam, Amelia and Sonja aren't exactly unfriendly.

Neither is Max, but that doesn't really count, since he's not exactly anything, no matter who he's sitting beside. Not nice or mean or happy or sad. He just walks around *being*, without seeming to notice anyone else. He hardly ever says anything. It's like he's lost in his own thoughts all the time. But it's strange. As different as he is, no one teases him. No one can be bothered with Max. There's no point. He just wouldn't notice or even care. Vanya has tried a few times, and Philip, too. They test him with a mean comment now and then, but nothing ever happens. Max might frown and look confused, as if he doesn't really understand what they said, but that's all. So they give up.

As everyone piles onto the bus, I find a window seat and immediately sit down and look out the window. That way I don't have to watch everyone avoid the seat next to me, their eyes stopping for a split second on the empty seat and then on me before they turn away quickly to find another spot. The truth is, it doesn't bother me that much anymore. I'm used to it. But I might as well not watch.

This trip was the principal's idea. He told us all he thought it would be great for both of the sixth grade classes to go on a trip together, that it would help us get to know each other and have a better sense of belonging. Maybe he should have thought of that when we started fourth grade together almost three years ago. Now there are just a few weeks left before summer holidays, and when we start seventh grade in the fall, the classes will be split up differently. I really wonder what he was thinking.

We're in the bus for what feels like forever. The towns get smaller and farther apart as we get deeper and deeper into the forest. We take a break at a rest stop, where we eat our packed lunches at picnic tables and argue about who has the best lunch. Who's got Coke, who's got cookies and who's got the best kind of yogurt.

The lunch battle gets everyone talking about what kinds of chips and candy they have, and the chip discussion lasts almost the entire trip. Adam, Dunja and Albin seem alone in the Lays camp, which makes me wonder if

Albin likes Lays chips because he also likes Dunja. The rest of the class is just about evenly divided between Ripples and Pringles, except for a few voters who are rooting for some weird brands that most people haven't even heard of.

Even when we're back on the bus, Philip goes on and on about why Ripples chips are the best, his voice getting louder and louder. By the time he's done, he's all red in the face, really upset that Emily, Cecilia and Frederick refuse to agree that Pringles are the most disgusting chips ever.

"What's wrong with you people?" he shouts. "They're not even real potato chips. They're just potato meal pressed together to make chip-shaped things! A billion identically shaped chips!"

"But who cares? They *taste* the best. Isn't that what counts?" Emily pipes up.

"Yeah, exactly!" says Cecilia, who loves agreeing with people.

In desperation, Philip turns around to look for someone who will agree with him. He sees me in the seat behind him.

"Oh, it's you!" he calls out in surprise, and then he lowers his voice. "Okay, Amanda. You know which chips are the best, don't you? Lays, Ripples or Pringles?

"Ripples," I answer, because it's completely true. "Sour cream and onion."

Philip's face lights up.

"Yes!" he shouts joyfully. "See, everybody? Ripples win!" And he reaches out his hand to give me a high-five to celebrate the victory.

He seems to have forgotten that my opinion doesn't exactly count for much. If I'd answered Lays, he probably would have remembered pretty quickly that I'm always wrong. He would have shouted, "See, everybody? If Amanda likes Lays, they must be disgusting!"

I can't help but laugh when I look at my palm, still red from his enthusiastic slap. How idiotic. A few hours ago he hissed that I had the world's most disgusting backpack, and now all of a sudden I'm great, just because I like the right chips.

Strengthened by his success, Philip conducts a study of the entire bus population. Armed with pen and paper, he runs around asking everyone, including Teacher, the chaperones and the bus driver, so he can settle the chip question once and for all. The results get him so excited that he grabs the microphone out of its stand next to the driver and turns it on.

Then he announces, "Ladies and gentlemen, the answer you've all been waiting for, what is the best kind of potato chips? I have conducted a scientific study, interviewing everyone, absolutely everyone on this bus." He makes a dramatic pause. "I'm starting from the bottom, of course, to makes this more suspenseful. In last place is Humpty Dumpty chips with one single vote. Then comes Sunchips with two votes, and Miss Vickie's with all of four votes. Okay, now it gets interesting. Lays gets just six votes! Pringles has a grand total of seven votes, and…" Philip pauses again and tries to do a drum roll. "The winner…with ten votes is…of course…the unbeatable, fantastic, absolute greatest…Ripples!"

All the Ripples fans applaud, even me. Teacher applauds, too, even though I heard her vote for Miss Vickie's. She seems impressed with Philip's comedy routine.

"Just like a real talk show host," she says to Dunja's mom, smiling one of her big fake smiles.

When we arrive at the wilderness adventure camp, it's already dark out, and we can't see much more than the outlines of the cabins where we're going to sleep. Teacher says it's been pouring rain up here for several days, but now the sky is clear and pitch black above us. I stand there in awe, gaping up at the sky. I realize I look silly and I try to close my mouth, but I can't. I've never seen so many stars before.

Vanya stands next to me, giggling.

"What's wrong with you? Did you sprain your neck or something?"

She looks up to see what I'm staring at. I can tell she's impressed, too, because she breathes in sharply and can't help letting out a little "Wow." But soon she manages to collect herself.

"Whatever!" she says, dragging her backpack into the nearest cabin.

———

As soon as we're all out of the bus, Teacher tells us that there are two bunk beds in each room, so we need to choose groups of four to share with. When Teacher mentions that we have to choose roommates, I go cold with fear. I know no one will choose me, and that whoever is forced to share with me will sigh loudly to show how much they don't want to. So I swallow my pride and lean over toward Emily, who sits next to me at school, and whisper, "Can I sleep in the same room as you?"

She looks at me, disappointed, but I can tell she understands. She quickly passes two little notes to Amira and Saga to check with them if it's okay. Amira and Saga look at each other and frown, but then they nod yes, hesitantly, first to each other, then to Emily.

Before we know it, our bags are unpacked and we're settled down for the night. I'm in a bottom bunk, beneath Emily, and I'm actually chatting away with the other three girls. We giggle and gossip and tell ghost stories and exchange candy and chips. Amira tells the story about the girl who was waiting in the car for her boyfriend when a crazy ax murderer came up and banged on the car roof, holding up the boyfriend's severed head. We've heard the story a thousand times before, but it doesn't matter. We shiver just as much anyway, maybe even more than the first time. After a while I tell a scary story, too, the scariest one I learned at Girl Scouts, the one about the killer who snatches babies out of baby strollers and eats them. I'm worried they're going to say it's lame and not scary at all, but instead Emily shouts, "God, how gross is that!"

And the others agree.

I feel so completely happy, and together we giggle and chat until one in the morning. They each go quiet one by one, their breath becoming deep and regular. Amira stops talking in the middle of a sentence, something about which guy in the class is cutest, and suddenly she's asleep.

I lie awake a bit longer, wanting to be alone and enjoy the happy feeling inside me. It feels like a big laugh is spreading through my belly and chest. I got to be part of this night, to share all the talk and laughter and candy, and nobody did or said anything to make me feel like I didn't belong.

Chapter Two

WHEN WE LEAVE OUR cabins in the morning, we're met by a man in green clothes and big hiking boots. He takes us on a hike to a beautiful clearing with a big fire pit in the center. We get to try lighting a fire using a flint and steel wool. I manage to create lots of sparks and one small glowing ember in the middle of the kindling, but it soon goes out. No one in the class can get a proper fire going with the flint, so the man, whose name is George, shows us how it's done with a few quick hand movements.

It's like magic. He just grips the steel wool in one hand and flicks his wrist, and suddenly a cascade of bright sparks lands in the kindling and starts glowing and crackling. Then he cups his hands around the nest of kindling and blows, gently and carefully. Once the embers have grown, he places some dry little sticks next to them in the fire pit and continues to blow, more steadily now, adding one little twig at a time. Everyone stands there, breathless, just staring at what he's doing.

When the first flame appears among the twigs, a cheer breaks out.

When the fire is burning well, George starts unpacking things from a big backpack. It seems to have endless amounts of room, and it's hard to believe that he had the strength to carry it here alone. He mixes flour, salt and baking powder in a small pail with a lid. He kneads the mixture into dough, using water that we fetch for him from a stream that runs through the clearing. We form the dough into thin sausage-shaped rolls that we wrap around sticks. Then we hold the sticks over the fire until the dough is cooked. I know it's just regular quickbread, but somehow it's still really exciting, and some of the people in the class have never tried it before.

When George unpacks butter, juice and cookies, the morning is complete. We mix the juice concentrate with stream water and drink up. At least most of us do. Vanya and some of the other girls refuse to drink the juice, even though George explains that the water from the stream is probably cleaner than the tap water they have at home. The girls look at each other and lift their eyebrows meaningfully, their "he's crazy" face.

But I'm happy. What a breakfast!

I sit between Amira and Emily, chatting and joking around with them. Right here, right now, everything feels okay. No one is looking at me with their usual mean eyes. Maybe it's because everything is a bit different than normal. We're in a different place, with new smells, new

tastes and new sounds. Maybe we become slightly different people when the schoolyard and the cafeteria don't
remind us of who we usually are.

But some things *are* just like always. As usual, Philip
and Andrew are acting stupid, throwing dough balls at
Vanya, and Vanya's scream sounds the same no matter
where she is.

"Stop, stop!" she shouts again and again, but I can tell
she doesn't want them to stop. She wants nothing more
than for them to keep the dough war going.

After breakfast, George pulls even more stuff out of
his bag. He hands each of us a plastic case, smaller than
a pack of gum.

"We're going to make survival boxes," he says. "Can
anyone guess what that is?"

Some people try to be funny, saying they're probably
boxes that survive extra long, or boxes made of a special
plastic that you can eat when you get hungry.

George smiles patiently. He's probably heard all these
stupid jokes many times before from other school
groups.

"Well, the plastic *is* actually important," he explains.
"It makes the box completely waterproof, and that's a
good thing for the matches we're going to put in there."

Then George pulls a bunch of small bags out of his
backpack. They're filled with matches, fishhooks and all
kinds of other stuff. Finally he grabs something he's kept
hidden under a bag, and looks at us jokingly.

"Do you know what this is?" he asks, opening his hand so everyone can see what he's been hiding.

A huge giggle spreads through the class, because what he's holding is a condom. Although it's still wrapped, it's unmistakably a condom.

"Um, yeah…it's a condom!" Andrew says finally, and sniggers even more.

"Exactly. Do you know what this is used for?" George asks.

Now Andrew and Albin are trying so hard to suppress their laughter that they have to lie down on the ground holding their stomachs.

"You guys are such babies!" says Cecilia with a sigh, although she's not doing that great a job at keeping a straight face either.

George is still holding the condom up, waiting for someone to answer his question.

"Of course we know what it's for!" Vanya finally bursts out. "You use it when you make babies, you know, if you don't want to have a baby!"

This sounds so funny that even Max starts giggling. I don't know if I've ever seen him laugh before. He brushes his dark hair from his forehead and smiles a big smile. Suddenly, he looks completely normal.

"Exactly!" says George again. "At least, that's what you normally use a condom for. But in terms of survival, we're actually going to need one for an entirely different reason."

He explains that in an emergency situation, you can use the condom to carry water because it's made of such strong material that it doesn't break, even if you fill it with several quarts. He even does a demonstration, using the stream water to show how much the condom can be filled up without breaking. It seems to stretch endlessly, and we stare in deep fascination.

Soon everyone has their own survival box, equipped with a condom, a box of matches, a fishhook, some fishing line and a little weight, five lemon-flavored fructose tablets, five weird tablets for purifying water, a needle and some thread, a sterile compress and an emergency candle. It takes a while before everyone finds a way to fit all the stuff into the small box and close the waterproof lid. It's like putting together a puzzle. It gets a bit easier, of course, for those who can't resist eating the fructose tablets. If I wasn't such a chicken, scared that George would yell at me, I'd try one, too. I can hear Cecilia enjoying one beside me and it's very tempting. But George looks like someone who could be very strict, so I don't risk it.

When we're done with our boxes George takes us into the forest to show us how to recognize some edible plants and medicinal herbs. I already know about most of them, since Mom and Dad taught Sebastian and me about them a long time ago.

Apparently it's all starting to feel too much like real school to some people, because they keep speeding ahead or slowing down to get away from the main group. Out of George's sight, Vanya and Cecilia try to scratch their names on a tree trunk using their fishhooks.

"Vanya and Cecilia = best F-R-E-I-N-D-S," they read out loud.

Max looks at the block letters carved into the bark, and raises his eyebrows.

"That's spelled F-R-I-E-N-D-S," he says, enunciating forcefully. Then he lowers his eyebrows to their normal position again. Vanya and Cecilia just stare at him, but he doesn't bother explaining. He just walks on by to catch up to the group.

When it's time to eat we all head back to the cabins. It turns out there's a cafeteria there, too, almost like at school, but much smaller. And you have to go get the food yourself. There's no adult there to dish it out. We serve ourselves as neatly as we can. I don't think anyone spills a drop. It's beef stroganoff and rice, and when I smell the food I realize I'm ravenous. I guess we didn't really get much to eat at breakfast.

I sit down next to Emily, without hesitating for once. I'm allowed, I think. I don't need to ask permission.

But when Emily looks up at me, I realize right away that I am mistaken. I guess that just because no one has been mean to me for the past twelve hours I've started imagining things, like maybe people like me. The disappointment in her eyes is obvious — I can tell she hoped it would be someone else sitting down beside her. Of course she doesn't say anything. Emily isn't the kind of person who would actually ask me to leave, but I can see that she's already sick of having me around all the time. As if she has suddenly remembered the way things should be. After all, it almost feels normal here, like we're back in the school cafeteria. And it's normal for no one to want me around. So I swallow all the happy words that I wanted to share and I eat the way I usually do, without a word.

As if to prove just how much of an idiot I've been, imagining that things would be different for me because we're here, Philip brushes past me, bending down and whispering in my ear, "Amanda, you look so incredibly disgusting when you eat."

He smiles and nods at me before he walks away so Teacher will think that we're friends, just having a nice chat. That's his specialty.

For the rest of the meal I chew so carefully that you can hardly tell I'm eating. I keep my mouth closed tightly the whole time so no crumbs can fall out, and I wipe my mouth and chin now and again, just to be safe. I drink my milk in tiny, tiny sips. I don't want to look disgusting. I might never be beautiful or look like a TV star, but at least I can not look disgusting.

People make stuff up about me all the time, saying things that I know aren't true. But this time, I'm not so sure. I try to remember what I was doing when Philip walked by, but I can't. Was I chewing with my mouth open? Did I have stroganoff sauce running down my chin? Or maybe I was making loud chewing noises? Maybe I really did look disgusting. I don't know. And that's why I eat the rest of the meal so carefully that by the time the lunch break is over, I've hardly eaten anything, and I'm not even close to full.

Chapter Three

AFTER LUNCH, it is time for the week's big adventure: white water rafting. The green and white bus comes back to drive us to a river a few miles away. When we get back on the bus, I know for sure that if I thought anything had changed, I was wrong. No one sits next to me. No one talks to me. For a second I consider sitting down next to Emily or Amira. Just doing it without asking, as if it was the most natural thing in the world. But I can't. I don't want to see the disappointment in their eyes.

The bus ride isn't very long, and after less than half an hour we arrive at the river. The river is wide and the water is flowing quickly, swishing in circles here and there from the current, but it doesn't look that scary. The six guides explain over and over again about how to steer, what to look out for, how to fasten the life jackets. They talk about how the water level is higher than usual because of all the snow we had this winter, so we have to be extra careful. At first I think they're saying all this to make it sound more exciting, but then they say, "Don't expect this to be like an adventure movie. There are hardly any rocks sticking up out of the water, and sorry, no waterfalls!"

They assign each of us to one of the three big rubber rafts that are tied to the dock, and we all get paddles and climb in. Of course, I get stuck with Philip right in front of me. He turns around and smiles sweetly, with his head tilted in that special mean way of his.

Andrew, who is on the boat behind ours, stands up and shouts to Philip, "Hey, Phil, check it out!" He pulls down the zipper on his life jacket, letting it dangle while he sings and dances, holding the paddle like a microphone. He jerks his hips as if he's in a music video on MTV. One of the rafting guides yanks him back down. She looks him right in the eyes and repeats what the guides said about safety and the high water. Then she makes him do up his life jacket again. We can see him blushing all the way from our boat, yet he still winks and grins at Philip, pulling the zipper on his life jacket up and down a few more times to show that he doesn't care about what the stupid guides say. I decide to forget about Andrew and turn back to face the front of the boat.

The guide at the front of each raft shows us one more time how to hold the paddle, how to put it in the water at different angles to steer the boat. We've already practiced everything on land, but now we get to try in the water, too, before they untie the boats from the dock.

Suddenly, we're off! The current grabs the boat, and we don't have to paddle at all to keep moving. We don't even really need to steer. We just use our paddles to keep the boat somewhere in the middle of the river. We're all trying really hard to put our paddles in the water at the exact right angles, just the way they showed us. People around me are breathing heavily from the effort, and my muscles are straining. I can tell that they'll be sore tomorrow.

I look over at Max, who's sitting to my left on the other side of the boat. He's looking intently at the whirling water, as if it's an exciting riddle he is about to solve. He's probably doing advanced mathematical calculations on the angle of his paddle as it hits the water's surface.

Then the current gets stronger and we start gaining speed. The raft sways slightly from side to side. Max looks like he's having a good time, but behind him, Vanya is staring straight ahead, terrified. She's trying to hold on to the edge of the boat and paddle at the same time. It doesn't work very well, and finally she decides to stop pretending. She puts her paddle down and holds on for all she's worth. Water has splashed up in her face, and the make-up she applied so painstakingly this morning has made black smudges around her eyes. That mascara that was supposed to give her such fantastic eyelashes doesn't look so good anymore.

The two guides in our boat look at each other over our heads. A tiny crease appears between the eyebrows of the guy sitting at the front. Right away I get the feeling that he's worried. Something isn't right. But we continue our journey and I soon forget my suspicions. It's going great! Of course there's nothing wrong.

But then the guide in front turns around again, and calls out something to the others. He's shouting through clenched teeth, as if he doesn't want us to hear, even though he has to scream to be heard over the sound of the river.

"There wasn't this much water yesterday when I did the trial run!"

"Yeah," the woman guide in the back shouts. "We're going way too fast! It must be the rain!"

Suddenly, I'm scared. I turn around to look at her, wanting so badly to see her smile, to be reassured that she's just kidding. But her face is serious.

"We should call this off!" he shouts, turning around again so she can hear him.

He shouldn't have done that. He shouldn't have turned around a second time.

His jacket glows bright red against the gray boat, the gray rushing water and the gray sky. He looks so strong with his hands firmly gripping the paddle. He looks like someone who knows what he's doing, who can't make mistakes.

But he should never have turned around.

He doesn't see the big fallen tree trunk in time — suddenly it's right in front of our boat. The tree is jammed between two boulders, and it's blocking the entire riverbed. I'm sure he would have been able to steer us away from the tree easily, if only he'd seen it in time...

Instead we slam right into the tree, and because both our guides have slowed down the boat to call off our journey, the other two boats are too close behind us. They don't even have a chance to stop. Instead they crash into us with full force, first one boat and then the next. I feel the collisions in my whole body.

Then I don't know anything anymore. Suddenly, I'm in the water. I cough and kick and wheel my arms around. I try to get some air, but water comes streaming down my throat instead. There's water everywhere. Icy cold, streaming water. I have no idea what's up and what's down, how or where to move to get to the surface.

But then my life jacket sucks me back up to the surface, and I can get air again. My body can't decide what it should do first, cough up water or breathe in air. For a long time it just feels like I'm going to suffocate. It seems like there's no water coming out or any oxygen coming in, but finally a few wheezing breaths make it down into my lungs, and the terror lifts a little. The whole time, the current pulls my body down the river, faster and faster.

When I manage to turn around to find out where I am, I see a group of bright dots in the water far upstream. That must be the rest of the class. They're so far away that I can't hear any sounds coming from their direction, even though they're probably all screaming their heads off. All I can hear is the water gushing around my head.

How have I ended up so far away from them? Why am I being pulled away so quickly by the current and they aren't? I can't think straight. The fear and the cold and the cough racking my body make my thoughts slow and thick, like syrup inside my head. I can hardly remember what happened. We were paddling, that I remember. And the guides looked worried. The guy in the bow turned around and called to the woman in the stern, and suddenly…

Right! The tree! Was I the only one who ended up downstream from the tree? Is the tree holding the others back, while the water is pulling me down the river with a current that seems to be growing stronger and stronger?

Feverishly I look around for a way to get to land, something to grab onto. All of a sudden I see something colorful right beside me, a blue jacket bobbing up and down in the water. Then I see a hood, and inside the hood… a face! It's Philip's face, although I can hardly recognize it, it's so distorted with fear. He spots me immediately.

"Amanda!" he screams. "Amanda! Amanda!" His voice sounds more scared than I've ever heard it. So scared he doesn't even care that I'm there to witness it, and that's saying a lot for Philip.

"Help me, Amanda!"

"I…can't!" I gasp in reply. When he hears me his face crumples even more.

"I'll try," I add, even though it's completely exhausting to try to overpower the rumbling river with my voice. I swim in his direction as hard as I can, but it's a huge challenge to swim against the strong current. For a moment I feel like I'm getting a little bit closer, but the next second he's farther away. The undertow pulls me back relentlessly. When at last I place a hand on his shoulder, I'm exhausted. My legs and arms are numb from the cold and the effort. As I hold on to him, my weight almost pushes Philip under the water's surface. I try to summon the energy to keep myself up on my own, but it's not easy.

We have to get to land. That's the one thing I'm sure of, but I can't figure out how it's going to happen. Philip seems as drained as I am, and I can't see a place where the water is calmer. I want to ask Philip if he has a plan, but I can't get any words out, my teeth are chattering so hard. The top teeth are rattling against the bottom teeth so violently, I'm afraid they'll break into pieces and fall into the river. All I can manage is a tired nod toward the shore. Maybe Philip can't even tell that I'm nodding. Maybe he thinks my tired head is just tossing back and forth in the water because my neck won't hold it up anymore.

But at last he tries to speak.

"Mmm," he grunts. It sounds like some kind of answer.

"Sh…sho…oore?" emerges weakly from my lips.

Again he squeezes out, "Mmm," and I think he's nodding.

So we swim as hard as we can toward the shore, trying to push through the cold, heavy water. Time after time my muscles cramp up, and I take what feels like my last stroke. At first it doesn't feel like we're getting anywhere, but then, suddenly, the shore is much closer. Even then, I'm so exhausted, the last stretch feels impossible. Luckily, a strong undertow comes to our rescue. It grabs us and throws us toward the riverbank.

The last thing I think before we hit the shore is that we're going way too fast. I see some big gray rocks coming toward me. Then I don't remember anything.

When I regain consciousness, I have no idea how much time has passed. I can hear the sound of the river clearly, yet I know that I've managed to get out, because although my clothes are still drenched, water is no longer tugging at me from every direction. I'm trembling violently and my whole body feels frozen. My muscles are weak and lifeless after the fight against the river.

I feel a strange weight around my waist, and open my eyes to see what it is. Something blue. Something blue and heavy. Philip's jacket is blue… so the heavy thing must be his arm. When I move my gaze higher up

I see his face, and it's just as miserable and shaky as mine.

"Are you awake?" he asks stupidly. "I guess you fainted. I pulled you up here." Then he remembers who I am and pulls his arm away hastily. "Sorry, but it's so damn cold, I thought if I lay close to you…"

"Well, of course you did," I say after coughing and clearing my throat a few times. What does he think, that I'm going to think that he likes me? How? When? When we were close to drowning and on the brink of death? Especially me of all people.

"That was good thinking," I say. "Thanks for pulling me up."

He smiles. Or at least I think it's supposed to be a smile. It's hard to tell with his lips trembling so badly.

"But now I feel like I'm going to freeze to death," he says, looking scared.

"Me, too," I say, and slowly, very slowly, the thought occurs to me that he's probably right. We're probably getting hypothermia. Okay, it is late spring, but it was already pretty chilly this morning and now there's a high wind, too. And we are sopping wet. We have to get out of here, dry up and find shelter from the wind. I know it's a question of life or death, and yet I don't see how I'm ever going to be able to stand up. My limbs feel like someone has emptied them of their life force, like deflated balloons. I can't feel my feet and hands at all anymore. And it feels like my brain has frozen into an ice cube. I can hardly think straight. If only the wind wasn't blowing so hard! I can feel it through my wet clothes, chilling me more and more by the minute.

"We have to get away from the wind, find some shelter," I say.

"In the trees," says Philip.

He's right, of course. We just have to drag ourselves a few feet up from the shore, and the dense woods will protect us. We try to get up. It takes forever just to get to our hands and knees. When I finally stand up, everything goes black. But after a moment I'm able to start toward the edge of the woods.

"We should keep moving," I say, once we've made it to the trees.

"Yeah, we probably should." Philip looks lost in thought. "I think I know which direction we came from this morning. I think I can find the way."

"Okay," I say. If I can stay on my feet, I'll warm up, and that's all I care about right now. I don't care which direction we go in.

"Are you coming?" he asks, his voice sounding eager all of a sudden.

"Okay," I repeat, pulling in a deep breath, getting ready to move my legs again. Philip goes first, and I follow. My feet thud like dead lumps against the ground. I have no idea where he is leading me. I can hardly keep my eyes open.

Branches hit my face. I see them coming toward me,

see them bending back when Philip brushes past them, but I'm too tired to hold my arms up for protection. I can't think. All my concentration goes into putting one foot in front of the other, again and again. It's a huge challenge just to walk without falling over, as if I were a little kid again. We walk and walk for what feels like forever. Eventually it starts to get dark.

A vague discomfort lurks somewhere in my mind, trying to tell me something. Does Philip know where he is going? Isn't there something I learned about staying in the same place when you're lost? Should we be moving around like this? Shouldn't we wait for…for someone to come and…I don't know. Too tired.

At last he stops.

"We won't make it today," he says.

"Sleep," is all I can muster in reply.

"Yeah! Sleep!" He sounds happy just thinking about it. But then he says, "But it's cold, do you think we'll be okay? My clothes aren't even dry yet. Are yours?"

"Nope, not even close," I say, brushing my hands against my clothes to feel if they're any drier. The cold layers of fabric stick to my skin, and I discover an unfamiliar garment — the life jacket! I still have it on! Despite how miserable I feel, I laugh.

"What is it? What's so funny?"

"We still have our life jackets on!" Philip's glows orange in the darkness.

But then I get serious again. "Pine boughs," I say.

"What?"

"Pine boughs."

"Yeah, what about them? What do they have to do with the life jackets?"

"Nothing. We have to gather some pine boughs to sleep on and to pile on top of us so we don't freeze to death."

"Okay." Philip doesn't sound convinced, but apparently he doesn't have any better ideas, so he slowly starts to break branches from the trees around us. I do the same. I don't know where the energy comes from. My fingers are stiff with cold and fatigue, so it's hard to get them to cooperate. The branches and needles leave small cuts on my hands and arms, but we manage to collect a big pile. Half asleep already, we spread half of the branches on the ground and use the other half to cover ourselves. It's prickly and lumpy with all the needles and twigs, but I hardly notice. I fall asleep right away, my cheek stuck on a lump of sap. I wake up over and over again during the night, chilled to the bone, but exhaustion wins out over the cold and I fall back asleep. A restless, shivering half-sleep, but still sleep.

Chapter Four

PHILIP MOVES CLOSER TO me in his sleep, and when I wake up he's curled up tightly against my back. But as soon as he wakes up he slides away.

Amazingly, bright sun is shining down on us through the trees. When I concentrate on feeling the sun through the stubborn cold that's eating away at me, I find it warms my skin ever so slightly. My clothes are also a bit drier. They're still damp, but at least they're not soaking wet anymore.

Philip is busy shivering and making "brrr" sounds. When he glances over at me, he bursts out laughing.

"You're got stuff stuck all over your face!" he giggles.

It's the sap. After a night spent sleeping on the lump of sap, it's now completely stuck to my face. I put my hand up to touch my cheek, and then my fingertips get stuck, too. Philip laughs even harder. Then a gust of wind blows my hair forward into my face, so I end up with a bunch of hair stuck in the sap. At first Philip's laugh sounds friendly, but then it's as if he remembers how things should be between us. I can almost hear his nice laughter turning into spite.

"You look like a total freak," he says maliciously. Maybe he thinks he needs to remind me who's in charge. So I don't go imagining anything's changed just because I happened to witness how wimpy he was when he was about to drown. Then he laughs again and says, "It really is a royal pain that *you're* the one I've got for company out here in the middle of nowhere."

I say nothing. What are you supposed to say to something like that? I wouldn't exactly have chosen Philip either, if it had been up to me to decide who I'd be stranded with. But if I told him that, things would probably get even worse.

When he recovers from his laughing fit, he says, "Hey, I just remembered, we have breakfast!" He shakes a little plastic box in front of my face, so close I can't even focus on it.

The survival boxes! With stiff but ecstatic fingers I find the box in my jacket pocket and open it. I don't even have time to get mad at Philip for deliberately shaking the box in my face. All I feel is grateful that he made the discovery.

Miraculously, everything inside the box is completely dry. I find the fructose tablets and unwrap one carefully. I gnaw off a small corner first, wanting it to last as long as possible. It's not exactly the world's greatest breakfast, but instantly my whole body is filled with pleasure as the wonderful sweetness spreads on my tongue and along the roof of my mouth. I can't control myself any longer — I pop the whole tablet into my mouth, and push it around and around with my tongue. I've never tasted anything so delicious. Not until this moment do I realize how incredibly hungry I am. Until now, all I've been able to think about is the cold and the exhaustion. I try to force myself not to eat all the tablets, but it's impossible. Greedily, I devour all five, until suddenly I remember what Philip said to me yesterday.

That I look so incredibly disgusting when I eat. My mouth stops moving, and I stare at him. Just now I must have looked more disgusting than ever, because I really wasn't thinking about anything but how wonderful it was to get something in my stomach. I was slurping and sucking like a pig to get the most pleasure possible out of those five measly tablets. But Philip seems not to have noticed. He's busy enjoying his own tablets at least as loudly as I was, and he just looks back at me and says, "Awesome!"

Still, I eat the last tablet as carefully as I can, barely moving my mouth, swallowing the dissolving fructose as quietly as possible.

"All right, I guess we should keep going then," I say when I'm done. I try to sound happy and confident, like someone who would never worry about looking disgusting when she ate or having the wrong kind of clothes or a backpack that came from the dump. Besides, I think, maybe Philip will be happy to continue leading our march out of the woods. If he has something to be proud of, he might not have time to think up nasty things to say about me.

"Um, yeah… sure," says Philip, but I can hear doubt in his voice. The words come out slowly, and he stares at the pine needles on the ground while he speaks. He sucks in his lower lip, and sits like that for a long time, quiet.

Then he says it.

"Um, actually… I don't think I really know where I'm going. I thought I did yesterday, I was sure I did, but…" He shrugs his shoulders, glancing at me. He looks as if he's waiting for me to start yelling at him. And really I should, but on the other hand I'm partly to blame, too. I thought we needed to keep moving so I followed him yesterday without any questions.

"I was so tired and cold and everything," he continues, "and I just didn't know what I was doing. It was like I wasn't thinking clearly. I just got it into my head that I knew exactly where to go. I thought I was so smart," he says, looking ashamed.

Even though he has reason to be ashamed, it feels weird. Weird that Philip is the one sitting here mortified in front of me, Amanda. If we're never found, it will mostly be his fault. That's reason enough to feel seriously guilty, for sure.

But still. This is Philip. Philip who hates me most of everyone. Philip who always comes up with such cruel ways to make my life miserable, in that pretend-friendly way so teachers suspect nothing. Philip who pinches my arms so hard he leaves bruises, and then turns around and makes gagging noises because he's touched me.

So I just say, "It's all right," sounding as nonchalant as I can. "I mean, it did seem kind of weird that you thought you knew where you were going. But we needed to move around, otherwise we might have died from hypothermia."

Philip looks relieved, almost grateful.

I continue, "So it's just a question of making our way back. That way it's easier for them to find us, and they're bound to be looking for us by now. I had a feeling that we should have stayed where we were from the beginning, but you seemed so dead certain, so..." It's not exactly true that I'd been thinking we should stay where we were the whole time, but making Philip feel bad is such a new and fascinating feeling, I can't stop myself.

He doesn't protest. He just sighs heavily and says, "Okay. Which direction did we come from?"

Nice question, coming from the person who got us here in the first place! I have no clue where we came from! It was pitch black. I was so cold and hungry I couldn't think straight, and I was so tired I was practically asleep. How could he think I kept track of where we came from?

Once I stop being irritated that he would ask such a stupid question, the gravity of the situation dawns on me.

"You don't know?" I say, slowly and clearly. I look him straight in the eyes, hoping he's just joking.

"Nooo," he murmurs. He clears his throat a few times to make his voice sound more confident, but then he gives up. "It was so dark…and cold…and I was so tired."

"Yeah, but you were up front deciding on the route!"

"I know." His voice is even smaller now, and I think it must be tears that are making him blink repeatedly. Did I just make Philip cry? Suddenly I don't feel like being mean to him anymore. If I did make him cry, he might never get over it, and that wouldn't do much to help us find our way home.

"It's not just your fault," I say. I try to sound friendly and comforting, but it comes out more like a harsh grumble, because now I'm scared, for real.

I try to remember where the sun was before it got dark yesterday, but all I can picture is a monotonous gray sky. There are no familiar markers around, just pine trees, stones and moss. And it was pitch black when we arrived. Maybe if it had still been light out, or if I hadn't been so tired, I would be able to remember the direction that big stone or this bent pine faced. The sunset, though, we should have noticed that even though it was overcast, right? I ask Philip, trying to get him to remember, but he shakes his head. He has no clue either. We sit there, dejected.

"So what are we going to do?" I say after a while. "We

should do something soon, while we're still alert from the fructose."

"Yeah, I guess so," he replies, but his face says he'd rather sit on this pile of pine needles and wait, even though he's starting to shake with cold again. "But what? What are we going to do?"

"Well…" I wave my hand uncertainly. "We'll just have to walk in some random direction. I think it looks clearer in that direction, sort of more open. What do you think?" I point, mostly to have somewhere to point, but now I think it might very well look brighter that way. A little bit, anyhow.

"I don't know. Maybe."

"Yeah, I don't really know either," I confess. "But we have to do something. I don't want the blame if we end up going the wrong way though."

"Me neither," says Philip. "Not again."

"Okay, we'll have to draw lots," I say, because I realize that neither of us has the courage to decide which way to go in case it's wrong. I reach out to a sapling beside me and pull off four new spring leaves. With my nail I carve one letter in each leaf: R, L, B, F.

"This means right, left, backward and forward," I explain. I cup my hands around the leaves and shake them up. Then I open my hands enough for Philip to pick one.

Solemnly, he chooses a leaf and reads, "Right. We're going right."

"Okay, then," I say, getting to my feet. "Let's get

going." And I start trudging ahead, trying to look more confident than I feel. Only when I start walking do I discover the blisters. Obviously, you're going to get blisters when you spend half a day walking in wet shoes, but yesterday I could barely feel my feet and had no idea how painful the blisters were. Now my legs want to buckle under me, and I have to bite my lip to stop from crying out. I guess I should check how bad they are, but it seems wimpy to stop before we even get going. Besides, I'm not sure I want to know. Maybe seeing huge blisters on my feet will just make me panic. Philip groans when he starts walking, too. I guess he's discovered the same thing. He doesn't say anything either.

Once again I think about what my parents told me to do if I ever got lost in the wilderness. Today, the memory is crystal clear. If you get lost, stay where you are. Otherwise you could end up walking in circles and exhausting yourself for no reason. More importantly, you might even walk into an area that's already been searched, a sure-fire way to stay lost.

But it's too late for that now, and we can't stay here in the middle of the woods. We have to find warmth and shelter, and find something to drink and eat.

We hike in silence for a long time. I'm not used to having normal conversations with Philip, and I can't think of what to say. Besides, neither of us wants to waste energy on talk when every step takes so much effort.

The sunshine that warmed us this morning disappears little by little. The sky turns dark gray, and then it starts to rain. It's a harsh, pelting rain, and it feels as if someone has turned on a freezing cold shower. Our clothes are soon drenched again, just when they were starting to dry out. My shoes make a slurping noise with every step, and water runs down my face. Philip's hair is plastered to his head like glue.

At some point we cross a small clearing filled with birches, and I grab a handful of the new leaves and start shoving them in my mouth, one after the other. Philip looks at me questioningly.

"There's some birch sap in these. And some vitamins, I think."

Hesitantly, he follows my example, pinching a leaf between his fingers and inspecting it warily before putting it in his mouth. He looks at me as if I'm crazy, but then he grabs a fist full of leaves and stuffs them in his mouth anyway.

"You don't have a knife, do you? Or anything else that's sharp?" I ask him.

"No, why?"

"We could tap some sap. It's really sweet. You cut a notch in the trunk, and it drips out."

Philip looks at the birch tree longingly and searches his pockets, but the sharpest thing he comes up with is the piece of metal that pulls up his zipper. He struggles for a long time trying to use it to carve into the bark, but it doesn't work.

I search my pockets one more time. They're empty, except for the survival kit and a pencil…and a hair elastic!

Pleased, I put my hair in a ponytail. What a relief! No more wet hair plastering itself to my face or getting stuck in the sap. By the time I'm done picking out the hairs that were already stuck, my fingers are sticky, too. If only I could wash up! But with what? Even though we look like we spent the day in the shower with our clothes on, the sap is just as sticky and gooey as before. I'd need hot water, at the very least.

As a last resort, I get the sewing needle out of my survival box, but when I try to use it to scratch the birch tree's surface, it breaks in half. Disappointed, I lean my head against the tree trunk for a few moments. More than anything, I just want to give up.

Everything is cold and wet and there's water everywhere, but my throat is burning with thirst. I grab hold of a small branch and lick the water droplets off the leaves. I don't care if Philip thinks it looks disgusting or crazy. The water droplets help just enough to get me going again.

"I guess we should just keep walking," I say gloomily.

Philip follows me, like he has all day. I know some tricks to make sure we keep going in the same direction. I might not be an expert, but I think I manage to avoid leading us in circles. And Philip trusts me.

"You know about this kind of stuff," he says, sulking.

It feels weird with him behind me, like he's taking orders. I decide where we're going and he follows.

The fact that I know about the woods and plants and stuff is one of the things that Philip and Vanya and all the others hate about me. Right after the adventure week was announced, Philip came up to me at recess and hissed in my ear, "You like that kind of boring crap, don't you? Stupid granola nerd."

Stupid granola nerd. That's what they think I am. For a while Philip even went around saying that I smelled because I spent so much time in the woods, but thankfully he got sick of that pretty fast.

One of the girls, Cecilia, lives really close to where the Girl Scout meetings are. She always reports back to the others when she's seen me "go and nerd out with the granolas." I seriously think she keeps track of when the meetings are and stands in the window looking for me, because she always knows when I've been to one. For a while I took long detours so I wouldn't pass her house, but in the end I felt so ridiculous and spineless that I started going straight past her house again.

And now Philip is walking behind me letting me decide on our route, just because I am a "stupid granola nerd." Now and then I can hear him sniffling so quietly that I have a feeling he's trying to hide it. I know that it's not a cold that's making his nose run. But I don't turn around to double-check.

Chapter Five

WHEN DUSK BEGINS TO fall, I'm close to giving up. I'm completely drenched and all I can think about is how hungry and thirsty I am. My whole body aches and my feet feel like two enormous blisters. Just then I see some light through the trees and I'm filled with hope. Maybe we're getting closer to the river. Maybe we've found our way back!

But no such luck. It's not a village either, or even a working farm. No, there's not a person in sight, but there is a big, dark blue lake and an open meadow spreading out in front of us. And there, between the pines and the lake, is an old dilapidated house in the middle of the clearing. It's pretty obvious that no one lives there anymore, since half a wall and part of the roof have caved in. But somehow, I feel safer all of a sudden. At least we're not the first humans ever to have set foot here. That's something. And there might be a road nearby so we could stop hiking around haphazardly. If there's a house, there must be a road, and a road has to lead somewhere.

Somewhere that there are people and food and warm, dry clothes.

I search all around the house, walking long distances in several different directions even though my legs feel ready to give out. But no matter how hard I look, there is no road. This house must have been abandoned eons ago. A hundred, maybe two or three hundred years, I have no idea. It looks ancient, like something from a pioneer village. Why would there be a road leading somewhere like this? I can't even see any paths between the house and the lake.

But I do find something else: a stream running into the lake with clear, fresh water. I sink to my knees and drink. I don't even bother to cup my hands. I just lower my face to the stream and slurp up the water in huge gulps. Philip throws himself down flat on the ground and scoops water into his mouth with his hands.

When we've drunk enough to quench our thirst, we both lie on our backs in the grass, breathing heavily, ignoring the rain that's still pouring down on us. We can't get any wetter than we already are.

"Should we stay here tonight?" Philip asks. "I don't think I can go any further."

"Yeah, let's stay here."

We look up toward the house. I wonder what's hidden inside. The whole place looks so ramshackle that I doubt that the roof even keeps any rain out. Anything left inside must have decomposed a long time ago.

"I wonder…" says Philip.

"What?"

"Oh, nothing, I was just thinking…well, I don't really believe this, but do you think that there might be something in there? I saw a movie once where these people found an abandoned house, and there was this old bed inside with a skeleton lying on it. It was really scary. I mean, I didn't think so when I saw the movie, but now…well, obviously I wouldn't be scared now either, if there was a skeleton in there, but still…" He gets tangled up in his own explanations and goes silent.

"No way!" I say, trying to sound brave. "You've seen too many horror movies. This house is as abandoned as it can get. That's pretty obvious, right?"

"Exactly," says Philip. "Although that might mean it's haunted." He realizes that once again he's said something that could make him sound like a sissy, so he adds, "Don't you think so? Doesn't it give you the creeps?" He's teasing now, as if he said all that just to scare me. But his voice sounds small when he continues. "Why else would people have deserted the house if it's not haunted?"

"Well, maybe…" I try, but I can't think of a good explanation. I sit up and wrap my arms around my knees. All of a sudden, I don't feel comfortable lying stretched out anymore. My eyes start scanning the area, searching for ghost-like shadows. Normally, this kind of stuff doesn't get to me. I mean, I don't even believe in ghosts! At least not when I'm at home in my warm, cozy bedroom, with Sebastian in the room next to mine, and Mom and Dad across the hall. If only it wasn't getting dark so quickly...

"No way!" I say again, mostly to convince myself. "Come on, let's go look. We can't just sit here in the rain. The house is probably just filled with old leaves. And cobwebs, maybe. That's probably the scariest thing we'll find in there."

I get up and start walking toward the house. Not because I'm really that brave, but because it feels good to be the daring one for a change, or at least the one who can pretend to be daring.

"Yeah, you're right," Philip says, trying to laugh.

When we get to the entrance of the house, I hesitate. The door is hanging on an angle, like it could fall on top of us at the slightest touch. I shudder as I nudge it carefully. It moves a half-inch, and nothing horrible happens. No monsters rush out, no skeletons rattle. So I place the palm of my hand flat against the decaying planks and shove the door open with one firm movement. It squeaks loudly, as if complaining about being disturbed.

Suddenly, there's movement inside the house. Something rushes around in the darkness and then heads straight toward us. I scream. I don't give a damn if Philip thinks I'm a wimp. Besides, he's screaming like a stuck pig, too. We spin around and bolt. Minutes ago we thought we couldn't take another step and now here we are running faster than ever.

The terrible thing from inside the house catches up with us and we stop dead in our tracks. Petrified, we stare as the black silhouette passes us and flaps away across the lake.

There is something familiar about it. Suddenly I burst out laughing. The relief is so immense I guffaw like a maniac. I even have to sit down. The sprint and now the laughing fit have knocked the breath out of me.

"What's wrong with you?" Philip hisses. He seems to think I've lost my mind.

"Pigeon," I laugh, gasping for air. "It was just a pigeon!"

Philip glances uneasily at our terrifying ghost, now no more than a dark dot over the lake. A smile twitches around the corner of his mouth.

"Are you sure?"

"Totally sure. I think I can recognize a pigeon when I see one!"

"Oh, you can, can you?" Now Philip is giggling, too. "Why did you run away then? And scream like a mad woman?"

"I was just trying to scare you, don't you get it? You big dork!" Even as I'm saying it, I regret it. But it's too late, the words have already snuck out of my mouth. Of course it's a joke, but I'm not the kind of person who gets to joke around with Philip. I just called Philip a dork. My laughter dies, abruptly.

"What's the matter?" Philip asks, still giggling. He's so

relieved to have escaped the horrific ghost pigeons that he's apparently forgotten to get mad at me.

"Um, just kidding. Yeah, I was really scared, too. Sorry I called you a dork. I was just joking." I look down at my hands, nervously pinching the knees of my wet pants.

"I know, I get it. Do you think I'm stupid or something?" Philip replies. "Of course I got that you were kidding! I was making a joke, too. You get to joke around with your frie…" Now his laughter stops, too. He hears how wrong it sounds to refer to me as a friend.

"…joke around with each other," he corrects himself, awkwardly. He sits down a few feet away, and we just sit there quietly in the rain for a long time. Not until it's completely dark does one of us speak.

"Okay, should we go in then?" Philip asks hoarsely.

"Yeah, I guess we should. But it's dark now," I say. I'm not exactly eager to go into the pitch dark house, even if the ghosts were just pigeons.

"What, are you scared? We have candles!" says Philip.

Right! The candles in the survival boxes! Feeling reassured again, we tiptoe back toward the house. I have no idea why we're creeping around except it seems to fit with the darkness, the smell of the woods, this mysterious house. We light our candles in the doorway. We use just one of our precious matches, anxiously protecting the unsteady little flame so it doesn't blow out before the wicks have caught fire. Then we look around.

The candlelight flickers, making all the shadows in

the room seem alive. The floor is nearly covered in decaying planks that have fallen from the walls and ceiling, some in pieces, some broken into a thousand brittle splinters. The walls look like they might fall apart at any moment.

The house just has this one room. Straight ahead of us is an old wood stove. It looks ancient. And pushed up against the far wall, there's a small bed.

Philip moves toward it slowly, one foot at a time. He's probably still thinking about the skeleton, scared he'll find one on the bed, the remains of someone who died there long ago. And when I see the grave determination on his face, I'm frightened, too.

As Philip approaches the bed, his breathing is shallow. He moves the candle back and forth over the cot. Then he reaches over slowly, slowly, to grab the corner of something grayish brown. It's an old blanket. Philip's whole body is trembling and the candlelight becomes more and more wobbly as he stands there, trying to find the courage to pull back the blanket to see what's hiding beneath.

Then he just goes for it with one big jerk that sends dust and dirt whirling around the room. His candle nearly goes out. I steal up behind him to see for myself, and when I reach him he shudders. We both search the bed thoroughly, holding up our candles for light, but there's no skeleton. Nothing else that scary either. Just leaves, pine needles and dust, and some small brown balls I think are mouse poo. Philip is still shaking like crazy, but he looks very relieved.

After the stove and the bed there's only one thing left to investigate: the cupboard. There are no tables or chairs, not even a stool. The cupboard is divided into two parts with a door at the top and drawers at the bottom. At some point it must have been painted blue and white. I can see the colors when I hold my candle really close. The latch has rusted onto the frame, so I have to pry at it for a while before it loosens and the door glides open.

Inside the cupboard, there are plates and cups, and a clay pitcher containing some wooden spoons, knives and a couple of forks. There are two iron kettles and a cast-iron pan that's so heavy I can barely lift it off the shelf. My stomach suddenly growls, loud and angry. I try not to focus on how hungry I am. Everything is covered with a thick layer of dust. The pots and pan are brown with rust, yet they seem to be better preserved than anything outside the cupboard.

Eagerly I turn to the drawers at the bottom. I guess they've swelled from the damp during the many years they were left untouched, because they stick when I try to open them. I'm forced to put my candle down on the bottom shelf and grab the top drawer with both hands. When I pull it open there's nothing but a few crumbs rattling around. The disappointment is crushing.

As Philip watches me with his candle raised, I pull out the second drawer.

I glimpse cloth, a big pile of it. I grab the top layer and pull it out. It unfolds into a dress, a worn, gray brown dress that feels cold from the moisture that has been trapped in the drawer all this time. A forgotten dress in a forgotten house in a forgotten forest.

I can't help holding the dress up to myself. It is so long and old-fashioned that its wide, sweeping skirt reaches my toes. I sway lightly back and forth. Even though the dress is torn and gray and looks so poor and pitiful, I feel like I did when I was little and used to dress up as a princess in my mom's grown-up dresses. Philip laughs at me, but I'm too curious about what's in the drawer to even care. When I continue searching I find an apron, a skirt and a blouse. The last thing I pull out is a dress that's even more worn than the first. It's so small it must have belonged to a child.

Gently I smooth the cloth with my fingers, feeling the uneven patches and the stitches where it's been mended. I lift up my candle and bring it closer to get a better look. This material is gray brown, too. Everything looks gray brown in this house, an indefinite color that must have been lighter once upon a time.

Something about the little girl's dress makes me feel like crying. I feel silly standing here getting sad about a piece of bedraggled old clothing, but I can't help wonder about it. Who used to wear this dress, so long ago?

Where did the little girl go? She must be a wrinkly old lady by now, or maybe she's already dead. Why is her childhood dress lying here, neglected and forgotten?

Philip obviously doesn't feel like waiting while I wonder about the child's dress. He puts his candle down and pulls hard on the next drawer, second from the bottom. It contains clothes, too, but this time men's clothes: a pair of pants and two shirts. One of the shirts is coarse and worn, and the other is made of a finer material. It must have been a dress shirt.

I can almost see the little family in front of me — a woman, a little girl and a man — the people who wore these clothes and who, for some reason, left them behind.

In the bottom drawer we find three wool blankets. Philip and I look at each other and break into an excited cheer.

"Yes! Yes! Yes!" he shouts.

Sure, the blankets are dusty, damp and so worn in places that you can see right through the wool, but when we've shaken them out and inspected them carefully, we decide that they are actually pretty clean. They do smell slightly of mold, but I'd rather be covered in mold than spend another night freezing. Not to mention the fact that we are even wetter tonight than we were last night. Even as we stand there, water is dripping from our clothes and shoes, forming muddy puddles around our feet.

I don't want to get the precious blankets wet, so I decide to wring out my clothes. I walk to one of the far corners, turn away and start undressing. I take off everything but my bra and underwear, and then start twisting my pants and shirt to get some of the water out. I would never have guessed that such small pieces of cotton could hold so much water.

At first I'm worried that Philip will think I'm weird or look at my body and find something to tease me about. But instead I discover that he's standing in the opposite corner wringing out his clothes, too. When I've made sure he isn't looking, I quickly take my underwear and bra off and wring those out as well.

When it's time to pull the wet clothes back on again, they feel ice cold, and the dampness makes them scratchy and almost impossible to get on. It's like they're glued to my skin.

When we're finally dressed again, we find a spot where no rain is coming in and spread one of the blankets out on the floor. We lie down as far away from each other as we can get. We turn sideways on the blanket to put as much room between our bodies as possible, so when we stretch out, our feet rest on the dirt floor. Then we each wrap one of the blankets tightly around our bodies, curling up our knees almost to our chins. Neither of us wants to use the blanket from the bed. It's much dirtier and more tattered than the blankets from the drawer. Sleeping in the skeleton bed doesn't even cross our minds. Besides, it would probably break in two the second someone lay on it.

For a moment I wonder if maybe I should still be worried about ghosts, but I don't even finish the thought before my eyelids droop. I'm way too tired for ghosts.

Chapter Six

DESPITE THE BLANKETS, I wake up shivering the next morning. It's a regular kind of shivering though, not the desperate kind when it feels like you're going to die. My clothes are much drier than they were the night before, and I can't hear any rain clattering on the roof. Although the sky outside the window looks gray, it's not raining. I sigh with relief.

I stand up and jump up and down to warm up while I look around the room, seeing it in the daylight for the first time. The room doesn't look bigger, nor does the daylight reveal any more interesting discoveries, yet it still feels like a completely different place. It's hard to believe that we thought the house was haunted last night, or that we thought we'd find old dried-out skeletons. The room is bright and it feels safe, even cozy. In the midst of all the decay, it is actually quite beautiful. There is something strange about this place, a kind of sadness resting over everything, an abandoned and forgotten feeling. But I'm not at all frightened by it anymore.

I am drawn back to the drawers and I pull the clothes out again, careful not to wake Philip. He's still asleep, his mouth open and a string of spit running down his chin. I don't know why I'm so fascinated by these clothes, but I want to hold them and run my hands over them.

In the light that streams into the room through the uneven windowpane, the broken-down wall, and the holes in the ceiling, I see that the clothes aren't all the same gray brown color. Almost, but not quite. The men's dress shirt is almost white. I want to wash these clothes. Not because it will do anyone any good, but because it feels like I should. Out of respect for the people lending us this house.

I start looking around for something to wash them in, and my gaze falls on the stove, the rusting, old wood stove.

Wait! We have a stove!

Of course I noticed the stove last night, but it's as if it didn't register how amazing it is that we have a stove! Right away I start listing all the things we'll do when we've fired it up. We'll be able to warm water for washing, we can cook whatever we find to eat...

The thought of food makes my stomach cramp up into a tight starving ball. All I ate yesterday were those five fructose tablets and some birch leaves. And the day before that, we didn't eat dinner, and I didn't even fill up at lunch because Philip said that stuff about how disgusting I look when I eat.

I put the clothes back in their drawers and start examining the stove more closely. At our cottage, the chimney sweep comes at least once a year to clean the stove. Mom and Dad insist that the house could burn down if the chimney gets blocked. There definitely hasn't been a chimney sweep at this house for years, if ever, and I bet the chimney is full of old twigs, leaves and other junk that could light on fire and shoot flames and embers onto the wooden walls. My spirits sink. It was such a great plan! Hot food!

No, I can't give up so easily. I carefully inspect the stove's hatches and brush off the dirt. I try to peer up the chimney, but of course I can't see a thing. Instead I go outside to take a closer look. Unlike most houses, which have small square chimneys sticking out of the roof, this house has a big stone chimney built right into the wall. Part of it has fallen in, and when I stand on my tiptoes I can almost see down into it.

I find a tree stump close by that the people who used to live in the house probably used to chop wood. I push my whole body against it and manage to tip the stump over onto its side so I can roll it over to the house. It's so heavy that when I try to push it upright, it keeps rolling back on its side again. Finally, after a few tries, I push it up next to the chimney. I feel weaker than normal, probably because I haven't eaten for so long, but that makes me all the more determined. The rotted old wood feels soft when I step on it but doesn't give way.

I look down into the chimney. I can see the opening at

the bottom that leads to the wood stove. It's not as full of rubble as I thought it would be. Just some old leaves and a wooden plank that has slid down from the roof. I bend over with my belly against the edge of the chimney and grope for the plank, grab it and pull it out. The leaves might catch fire but I don't think that will matter. I inspect the chimney wall but can't find any cracks or openings where embers might escape to light the house on fire.

After I'm done with the inspection, I gather some dry branches and a big pile of dry bark, which I pull off a fallen birch down by the lake.

By the time Philip awakens, the fire is crackling cozily in the wood stove, and I've had time to warm some water and finally wash away the sticky spot of sap on my face. The fire smoked terribly at first and I had to start again a few times with new twigs and birch bark, but Philip slept through the whole ordeal. All he can see now are the leaping flames of a big warming fire — I've left the stove door slightly open so he can get the full effect. I'm very proud that I was able to fix everything up so well. More than anything I want to smile a big boastful smile, but instead I try to look as if the fire is no big deal.

Philip doesn't say anything, but I can see that he's impressed and happy. Even though he turns his eyes away from the stove quickly, like he doesn't care about the warmth spreading from it, it's enough to have caught his first surprised, awestruck look.

I casually lift the lid off one of the pots on the stove,

which I worked long and hard to scrub clean of rust. There's nothing in the pot to get too excited about, really, just some pale green pine shoots in hot water. Still, I can see Philip's eyes pop open greedily when I serve him some in one of the cups I've washed in the stream.

"Are you sure these are edible?" he asks sourly. The unpleasantness cuts through another, warmer tone in his voice, the happiness at having a hot drink in his hand.

"Of course you can," I say. "You don't have to eat the shoots if you don't want to, but drink the water. It's filled with nutrients."

"Are these pine needles?" he asks suspiciously.

"Yeah, they're pine shoots, the new needles that grew this year. They're much softer than the old ones, so they won't prick you."

I feel like adding, "Didn't you know that already?" but judging by his mood I'm guessing that might get him into a huff.

He guzzles the drink so fast he burns his tongue, and then he pours himself some more. I go a little slower, blowing on the pine tea before drinking, savoring every sip. After such a long time with nothing to eat, it tastes wonderful, and I almost start to feel a little full, even though there can hardly be much nutrition in the bland pine water. But right now, it feels like a wonderful, nourishing soup.

"It's…" Philip starts, but then he interrupts himself.

"What?" I ask.

"Whatever, it's good, that's all. But that's probably just because I'm so incredibly hungry."

All of a sudden I'm furious. I know he's the one who gets to be mean to me, not the other way around. That's the way it's always been. But it's not fair. I struggled all morning while he just lay there sleeping, and now he can't even admit that he's happy about it, even though I can read it on his face.

I clench my teeth and with a completely calm voice I say, "Yes, I'm sorry. How stupid of me to think you'd want to drink something so disgusting. Why don't you go ahead and make your own yummy breakfast instead."

Then I take the cup from his hand. Slowly, I unwrap his fingers from around the mug, and he's so shocked he doesn't even resist. I drink what's left in the cup, ignoring the burning sensation in my mouth. When I've swallowed the last sip I don't dare look at him.

It's never occurred to me before to do something like this. Normally I don't talk back even when I know he's wrong and I'm right. Not because I don't have the guts, but because it's just so much work. Now that it's just the two of us, strange ideas fly into my head every five minutes. I feel like teasing him, coming up with evil jabs to make him feel dumb. It feels so great that he's constantly thinking about how stupid it was of him to get us lost. I have to fight the urge to remind him, to make him feel even more ashamed.

And now, now I've even gotten mad at him.

And this time I can't pretend that I didn't mean it or that I was kidding.

Is he going to hit me? He never has before, but maybe this time I've made him so angry he'll explode.

Finally he mumbles, "Sorry about that." He doesn't sound very friendly, but it seems like he means it.

I can't believe my ears. Sorry is the obvious thing to say. Anybody would apologize for what Philip just did, but Philip isn't anybody.

I glance up at him. He's staring sheepishly at his hands, picking at the blanket that is still lying over his knees.

"That was a stupid thing to say. You've fixed everything up really well," he continues. And after a little pause he even says, "Thanks."

I feel like I've landed on another planet. Embarrassed, I pour the last bit of tea from the pot into his cup and hand it to him.

"That's all right," I mumble, and then there's a long painful silence. Philip tries to make his tea last as long as possible, so he has an excuse not to talk.

Finally he says, "So what are we going to do now?"

"I don't know. I really don't know."

"I guess we can't find our way back, can we?" he says. "Not to the river or the camp."

"Nah," I agree. "There's no point in wandering around aimlessly. I've heard you're supposed to stay where you are when you get lost so that the people looking for you will have an easier time finding you. I think it's so you don't go into areas where they've already looked or something."

"I've heard that, too," Philip says.

Silence again, but this time it's not awkward. Just a little moment of quiet so we can figure out our thoughts. It feels weird to have admitted it. We're lost. Now that we've said it out loud, it feels so final. As if we hadn't been lost for real until now.

"So we're staying here then?" he asks.

"Yeah, I guess so," I say, and it feels so good. I can't even think about what it would be like to keep going for yet another day — even if our clothes *are* almost dry — without knowing when we'd see food or water or a house again. And with these huge blisters.

It's strange, I already like this house a lot. I wouldn't want to leave the blankets, the stove and the big pot. For some reason I'm attached to the other things, too, even the ones we really have no use for: the bed, the clothes, all the stuff that contains memories of the people who used to live here. If we left their house behind, I would miss the little family that I've never met.

"Should we try to make some kind of SOS signal?" Philip asks. "I mean, something that the people looking for us can see from far away. There are people looking for us, aren't there?"

"Of course they are," I say, trying to make my voice sound more sure and calm than I feel.

They are definitely looking for us. But how will they find us here? They're probably searching for our bodies in the river, assuming that we've drowned. But I don't say that to Philip. Not because I think he hasn't thought of it already. He's probably figured that much out for himself. Mostly it's so I don't have to hear myself say it. Saying it out loud would make it even more true.

Instead I say, "Great idea." Because it is, actually. "If they...I mean, *when* they search the area, we have to help them find us. It's good that we've got the stove burning, so they will see the smoke coming from the chimney. We should keep the fire going all the time. That way we won't waste matches either. And it'll keep the house warm."

"And maybe we should hang something up high where they can see it. Something bright so they can see it from far away," Philip suggests.

We look around the room at all the faded brown and gray stuff wondering what we could use. Our eyes fall on the bright orange life jackets. We nod to each other. Those will do the trick.

Philip looks at me. I can see that he wants to say something, but he's having a hard time getting it out. He sits there for a while, looking again and again like he's going to speak, but nothing comes out. I want to ask what he's trying to say, but that would probably make him hesitate even more. So I wait, not wanting to ruin the brittle friendliness that has grown between us.

Finally he says it. "Hey, Amanda... um, you're really outdoorsy. I mean, you know a lot about the woods and all that stuff. And that's really great. Because I don't know a lot about that stuff. So, um, do you know if there are any other things we can eat? Could you show me?"

I'm not surprised that that was hard for him to say. It must be a huge blow to have to learn things from me, the "outdoorsy" one.

At first I'm tempted to say that considering how *nerdy* he thought it was to like the woods, he's on his own... but I leave it alone. Not getting along out here would be pretty rotten. Not that we're becoming great friends exactly, but at least we've declared a kind of ceasefire.

So I answer, "Yeah, for sure. I'll show you."

Chapter Seven

THE FIRST THING WE do is hang the life jackets. I climb to the top of one of the smaller apple trees beside the house. Being surrounded by hundreds of apple blossoms is a pretty amazing feeling, and the delicate leaves flutter soothingly in the air, still crinkled from having opened so recently in the spring sun.

Again I think about the family that used to live in the house. Did they plant these trees? Did they think about how beautiful the apple blossoms were in spring? Or did they work so hard that they didn't have time to think about those kinds of things? Did the little girl climb up here and sit in the tree, surrounded by flowers and leaves? Did she also feel the rough bark under her hands like I do now?

The top branches are thin and weak, and it's kind of scary when they sway as I grab hold of them to pull myself up. I don't really want to climb to the very top, but Philip and I have agreed that the apple trees are the perfect place to mount our SOS signals. For a while we thought about whether we should put them where they could be seen from the ground, in case people were to pass by on foot, or whether they should be most visible from the air, in case they were searching for us by helicopter. In the end, we decided on a compromise. We'd put one life jacket where it would be visible from the ground, and the other one would go someplace where it would be visible from above.

From my position in the tree I can see that Philip has chosen a small birch that stands slightly apart from the birch grove, alone in the middle of the clearing between the house and the lake. He wraps his life jacket around the tree trunk and uses the buckle and zipper to attach it to the tree. It's the perfect size, clearly visible from every direction.

Very carefully, I tie the straps from my life jacket on to the tree so that it's spread out across the uppermost branches with the orange side facing up.

When we're done with the life jackets, we collect a big pile of wood to help us keep the stove burning. Then we sit down to catch our breath. Everything is such an effort when you're so hungry.

"We could write SOS, too," I suggest. "I think I read about that in a book."

"What do you mean, write?"

"Well, you write it with stones, on the ground. You arrange the stones so they form huge letters that will be noticeable from the air."

"Awesome!" says Philip. "But if we're going to drag stones around I have to have something to eat first. I'm so hungry that I'm starting to feel dizzy."

"Me, too," I say.

"But what can we eat?"

"Nettles!" I say.

"Stinging nettles?"

"Yes."

"You can eat those?" Philip sounds anxious. "Don't they sting?"

"Not when they're cooked," I say. I'm tempted to tell him that even normal non-outdoorsy people make nettle soup for dinner in the spring. But I say nothing.

We start looking for nettles. Several small bunches are growing around the house. I had noticed them earlier. They're small and delicate, perfect for nettle soup. Despite the fact that we don't have any spices, just nettles in hot water seems like a dream right now. I pull my sweater sleeves down as far as I can, grab the nettles with my protected hands, and collect them in my sweater, which I've pulled up to form a little sack in front of my stomach.

When we're done, we empty our harvest into the pot. It actually looks like we've got quite a bit. Then when I go out to the stream to collect water, I spot some small, yellow flowers. Spring onion! I have no idea if you can actually eat spring onion. I've never thought about it before. For me it's always been a flower that makes me happy because it means spring has arrived. Now it makes me happy because it's an onion. Can you eat all onions? Didn't I hear that somewhere? Or was it that no onion species are edible? No, that can't be it, you can eat chives, and of course you can eat the onions that you buy in the supermarket. But spring onion? It's more of a decorative plant, isn't it?

I get down on my knees and carefully dig up one of the plants. The root does look like an onion. A small, dirty, oblong onion, but still.

So I decide to bring them in with me. I know it's really stupid to eat something you're not sure is safe, but onion in the soup would be so good! And besides, I have to admit that I want to impress Philip. Silly and childish as it is, I really want to stroll into the house and calmly say, "I found some onion, too, by the way." I want to see the expression on Philip's face when I chop them up and drop them into the pot. Philip, the guy who thought there was nothing to eat around here!

So I do just that. I stroll into the house saying, "I found some onion, too, by the way."

I chop them up using one of the knives I found in the clay pot from the cupboard. Even though I've scrubbed it like a maniac, it leaves traces of rust on the chopped onion. Raising one of the onion halves to my nose, I smell it carefully. Yes, it does smell like onion. Normal, edible onion, plus maybe another more flowery scent, but mostly onion.

It turns out to be the best soup I've ever had. But neither one of us is very full by the time we scrape the last drop out of the pot. And now, worry is gnawing away inside me. What have I done? What if I've poisoned us? What if we both die? At the very least we might get stomach problems, and we might die from *that*, since we're here without access to medicine or anything.

At least our energy is somewhat restored by the food. Before we start collecting stones for our SOS sign, we cut notches into three birch trees so we can collect sap using the three cups we found in the cupboard. I carve grooves into three wooden sticks, not the easiest thing to do with the dull, rusty old knife. I end up with three sticks with little indents at the bottom, but they'll do. I wedge the sticks into the notches, and place a cup below each of them, and soon enough the sap starts dripping. This is the perfect time of year to collect the birch sap, when the leaves have just come out. Not that the sap is dripping quickly. It's just a slow, slow dribble, but of course we don't have to stand there watching. I'm surprised at how good it feels to see Philip watching me, fascinated with what I'm doing.

"Should we put the SOS stones on the slope down by the lake?" he asks.

"Yeah, that'll be good. That area is quite level, and the grass isn't as high there as it is in the meadow," I say.

We find what appears to be the remnants of an old stone wall near the woods, and we spend the rest of the day heaving and rolling the stones toward the lake. Before long, we're exhausted and covered in dirt and little cuts and scrapes. I feel bad about dismantling a wall that someone has obviously worked so hard to build, but it can't be helped. We need the stones.

As evening approaches, we've collected enough rocks to spell SOS in huge letters that are twice my height. The only thing that worries me is that maybe they're not visible enough. They're so gray, they almost melt into the background. I guess all we can do is hope.

We go back to the birch grove and peer into the cups, curious to see what's happened. They are half full! We each take a cup, and Philip shares the third cup's contents equally between us. He measures and pours so precisely that I have to chuckle.

"Do you have any brothers or sisters?" I ask.

"Yeah, two sisters. One older, one younger. Why?"

"You're dividing it up so fairly. It looks like you've had lots of practice."

"What about you?"

"I've got a younger brother, Sebastian," I reply. All of a sudden, my eyes are burning. Sebastian! When will I see him again? Will I get to hug him and kid around with him again?

"Cheers!" says Philip and lifts his cup. "Cheers to brothers and sisters," he adds, solemnly.

"Cheers to brothers and sisters!" I answer, and we bring our cups to our mouths. The sap tastes wonderfully sweet, with a fresh grassy flavor. Philip smacks his lips in astonishment.

"This tastes amazing!" he exclaims.

I feel so satisfied, as if even the delicious taste was my doing. We put the cups back under the trees right away, so as not to miss a single drop. Then we barely make it back to the house in time to crawl under the blankets, we're so tired.

My whole body aches from fatigue after hauling all those rocks. Still, I can't fall asleep. I just lie awake, worrying. The onion. What if it was poisonous? It was just a small plant. But you're not supposed to eat flowering plants without knowing what they are. You can't buy that type of onion... If it's safe to eat, why have I never seen it in a grocery store?

Imagine if I'm the cause of both of our deaths, out here in the wild.

I try to figure out if I'm feeling strange. This turns out to be difficult, because of course I feel strange, for all kinds of reasons. Hunger, exhaustion, fear, and I don't know what else. So how am I supposed to tell if I've been poisoned? I concentrate on my stomach and try to ignore the curling pain of hunger to see if I feel any other kind of pain. Is it grumbling more than it should be in there? I prod my belly with my fingers, as if I could feel from the outside whether I've been poisoned. The only thing I notice is that it feels flatter and emptier than usual.

I look over at Philip, but he's already asleep. Or...

He's so quiet! I'm not sure if he's breathing. What if he's already dead? What if he's just been lying there silently next to me, dying! I bend over him, listening for his breath, searching for some sign that I haven't poisoned him. But it's so dark I can't even tell if his rib cage is moving.

My ear is almost touching his face, listening frantically for a sign of life, when he snuffles loudly and turns in his sleep. I jump backward and my whole body tenses up. Lying down again, I try different positions: my side, my back, my stomach. Maybe stomach pains and poisoning are more noticeable if you're lying in a certain position? I listen for Philip's breath, and the whole time I'm trying to tell if I feel dizzy or nauseous. But nothing's different, except that I become very aware of how mind-bogglingly hungry I am.

Food is the last thing I think of before I fall asleep. Tomorrow we've got to find more food.

Chapter Eight

THE FIRST THING WE do the next morning is run around emptying the cups of birch sap, which have almost filled up overnight. The sap doesn't exactly fill us up, but I think I feel more awake afterward. We sit down with our backs against a birch tree, soaking up the sun, which has finally broken through the clouds.

"Can we wash the blankets today?" I ask. "They smell terrible. And it looks like good drying weather."

"Sure we can," says Philip emphatically. Apparently he doesn't think they smell great either. "But what if they're still wet when we go to bed? We'll freeze."

"Yeah, that's true. But we can wring them out really well. And maybe we can try drying them over the stove?"

Philip weighs the alternatives. Sleep with a half wet blanket or endure the moldy smell for one more night…

"Okay, I guess we'll wash them," he decides.

"I've been thinking we should wash the clothes, too, the ones we found in the house," I say.

"What for?" he asks, and I don't know how to answer him.

I have no good explanation for why I would want to wash the clothes, and I regret that I even said anything. I can't very well say that I have, for some strange reason, started to feel close to the family that lived here long ago, people who probably died long before we or even our parents were born.

Finally I make something up. "Well, I thought we could wear them if we start getting really cold."

"All right... maybe," says Philip. "But finding food is probably even more important. I'm starting to feel really weird from being hungry for so long. My hands have gotten really cold."

"Mine, too," I reply. My hands really do feel like a couple of ice cubes, even with dry clothes, a warm stove and blankets.

"Should we look for more nettles?" Philip asks. "We picked most of the ones around the house yesterday."

"Yes, we can do that, but I have a few other ideas, too," I say, and I can't help sounding mysterious.

"Like what?"

"You'll find out soon enough," I say, teasing.

"Oh, come on! Can't you see how curious I am?"

"Okay, okay. Well, I've looked around, and there's actually lots to eat."

As soon as I say that I feel ashamed about the onion

yesterday. I don't think we're going to die, since neither of us has noticed anything wrong yet, but still. That was a really stupid thing to do. Especially since there are a ton of plants here that I'm sure we can eat safely.

Philip looks around suspiciously, trying to find anything that looks edible. He doesn't make any silly comments about the Girl Scouts or my granola nerd family though. He just searches and searches, and when he comes up empty-handed, he shouts, "I give up! Tell me what it is!"

"Well, down there in the lake there are two kinds of edible reeds: pickerel weed and wapato. Both of them have edible roots. And there are probably more nettles, and a plant that looks a bit like nettle called curly dock. The leaves from those are also edible, although they taste a little bitter. And you can cook fiddleheads, too, if we can find any. Those are baby ferns. And those plants over there, they're Queen Anne's Lace. You can cook them up and eat the roots and the leaves. Look, there are tons of them. They're supposed to be pretty tasty, actually."

"Shit!" says Philip. "There's more food than we could possibly want! Let's get started right now!" He gets up eagerly and runs toward the lake.

"What about the blankets?" I call after him.

"Those can wait, can't they? We need food now!"

I follow him down to the lake.

Harvesting pickerel weed and wapato roots with your bare hands is not easy. We tug, yank and dig into the sand and mud where they grow. Smelly, sticky mud gets lodged under my fingernails, and my pant legs get soaked even though I've rolled them up over my knees. At last we're done. We're sweaty and filthy, and our feet and calves are frozen, but we've got a whole pile of reed roots. We rinse them in the stream, using our knives to scrape off any parts that look discolored.

Back in the house, we pile the roots into the pot. The fire has gone out while we've been busy harvesting food, and we're forced to use the matches again. To conserve matches, we light one of the emergency candles. This way we only need to use one match, lighting the little starter twigs directly from the candle. I make sure to put on a second pot to boil, this one filled with just water, since we're planning to do some washing.

It takes a long time for the roots to cook. Now and again we poke them with a knife to see if they're ready. We should probably be using the time to look for more food or collect wood or do something useful, but we're too weak with hunger and fatigue after the past few days of hard work and little sleep. So we sit down close to the stove to absorb the heat from the fire.

"Mmm… McDonald's," says Philip.

"Yeah! Quarter Pounder!" I reply.

"Nope. Big Mac all the way," he says longingly.

"Tons of fries."

"And ketchup."

"A milkshake," I continue, my mouth watering.

"Yes, strawberry!" he says.

"Pizza!" I almost shout, as I picture a huge, delicious pizza, smothered with melted cheese, imagining the overwhelming aroma of spices and oil.

"Holy crow," Philip moans. "With ham."

"Yeah. Or pepperoni. Or, oooh...bacon!"

"*Crispy* bacon." Philip says it slowly, as if he is trying to savor the bacon taste as the words roll around in his mouth. "With fried eggs."

"Roasted chicken. Deep-fried shrimp."

"Meat sauce with spaghetti," says Philip next. "A big pile of meat sauce."

"Chips!" I suggest.

"Ripples," says Philip.

"Sour cream and onion," I continue, and we burst out laughing as we remember the chip discussion on the bus.

Now that we've started thinking about snack food there's no stopping us.

"Popcorn. And peanuts."

"Beer nuts, with that crunchy layer on the outside," suggests Philip.

His mouth is moving, as if he's imagining that he has the nuts in his mouth.

"Chocolate! Snickers, Skor and Twix!" I say.

"Caramilk."

"Gummy bears, M&Ms, Tootsie Rolls, black licorice!" I rattle off, the saliva running down my gums, making me swallow a few extra times.

"Nah, not licorice," protests Philip. "Black licorice is so gross. I'd rather eat roots and birch sap than that stuff."

"Seriously? I love licorice," I say, dreaming about mountains of candy. "Licorice babies, black balls, oh, and those soft licorice gummies! Wow, those are almost the yummiest things ever."

My stomach yearns so intensely for all the delicious things we've been mentioning that it feels like it's about to turn inside out in protest. I have to squish into a ball and put my arms around my middle.

Philip dreams on. "Cinnamon buns. Apple fritters. Chocolate cake. Coke. Mountain Dew. Root beer."

He sighs deeply and confesses, "Right now I could kill someone for a glass of root beer. And it's not even my favorite soda."

"I could kill someone for one single piece of licorice," I say.

"You're crazy," he says.

Philip used to say that all the time. He said it so I would know what a loser I am. But this time it's different. It's not the usual, nasty voice. This voice has laughter in it, but no meanness.

I think harder about that for a second. Suddenly it hits me that Philip is not behaving the way he usually does. He hasn't been mean for, well, more than a day. In fact, he hasn't been mean since yesterday morning, when he apologized for not acknowledging how pleased he was with the breakfast I'd made. He's acting like I am a normal person who he can talk to and joke around with. Of course, he doesn't have a lot of choice out here in the wilderness, but still.

I can't stop a ball of laughter from forming in my stomach. Somewhere inside all the hunger cramps is a contented laugh.

Philip gets up to poke the roots in the pot again, and this time he says, "You know, I think they're finally done."

I get up and prod with the knife as well, and they actually do feel reasonably soft. They're even more shriveled than the overcooked potatoes they serve in the cafeteria. Yet my mouth waters, they look so incredibly delicious. Frantic with hunger, we heap the roots onto the worn, pale blue porcelain plates. Then we dig in so enthusiastically that we both burn our tongues and have to spit out the first bite so we can gulp mouthfuls of cold stream water out of our cups.

When I've blown on the next bite enough to cool it down, I stuff it into my mouth, and the roots actually taste pretty good! Maybe not as good as the burgers and fries that we've been dreaming about, but still. We eat and eat, and eventually we're full for the first time since we fell into the river. Really full, the kind of full where we have to take long, deep breaths.

Chapter Nine

WE WALK OUTSIDE AND sit down with our backs against the house. Sitting in the sun, with a warm wall behind me, it feels like a summer day. I'm close to falling asleep when Philip says, "I wonder if they'll find us."

Instantly I'm awake. *I wonder if they'll find us.* It's the first time one of us has dared to speak the words aloud. Philip, like me, must have thought about it a million times already, but we've both kept quiet. I don't know what to answer, because I really don't know what I believe.

"Yes, I think they will," I say in the end. "They know what they're doing, you know, the police and stuff." But deep inside I wonder. If that's true, why haven't they found us yet? This is the fourth day, if you count the day we fell out of the raft.

"But what if they think we're dead?" Philip asks.

"I know," I say. "I've wondered about that, too."

"And what if they're just looking for our bodies?"

"Yeah, well, they won't find our bodies, and then they'll figure out that we're alive and start looking for us, right?" I don't mean for it to sound like a question. I want to be dead certain to keep us from getting any more frightened, but the words form a question all by themselves.

"I guess they will," says Philip. But he doesn't sound very sure.

We sit there for a while in silence, each of us preoccupied with our own thoughts.

Then I say, "I'm scared."

I don't know why I say it. This whole time I've been fighting not to show Philip when I'm afraid, so he'll think that I can cope with everything, that I'm strong and can handle anything. But I can't deal with it anymore. I can't deal with pretending to be something that I'm not. Because it really isn't true. I am scared.

Philip looks at me for a long time, and then he says, "Me, too. And I'm homesick. I'm so homesick." And then come the tears. They pour down his cheeks, and he does nothing to hide them.

I sit there looking at Philip's tears dripping onto his chin, listening to his sniffling. It's all so weird. Never in a million years did I think I would experience something like this. But what I think about most is not how strange it is to see Philip cry, but how much I wish I could cry, too. It would be such a relief. Maybe if I was with someone else, someone other than Philip, I'd be able to. Not that I think that this new Philip sitting here, his jacket wet with tears, would make fun of me if I cried. But I've gotten so used to shutting everything inside me so he and the others won't find anything new to tease me about. I have to keep the tears inside. As always.

"I miss home, too," I say. "I miss my brother, my dad and my mom." The lump in my throat grows.

It's so strange that it would come out now, all of this. When we were at our coldest and hungriest, neither of us had time to miss anyone or feel sad. We were so busy trying to find warmth and food and somewhere to sleep that we had no time for tears. But now that we're warm and full and almost well rested, all the terrible thoughts have caught up with us.

Now that Philip has started crying, all kinds of stuff comes spilling out. He tells me about his worries, fears and homesickness, as if he can't stop himself.

His guilty conscience also kicks in. Suddenly, between sobs, he says, "Amanda, I'm sorry!"

He doesn't need to explain what he's apologizing for. We both know. I want to answer that it's okay, that it doesn't matter, but that would be a lie. It's not okay, and it does matter.

I could say that I forgive him, I suppose, because that is true. It's not okay, but I can forgive him. I feel like it's not exactly his fault. He's just been too stupid to realize how much he's hurt me. But it would sound so weird, so formal somehow, to just say, "I forgive you."

So instead I say, "Uh-huh." I stretch my hand out awkwardly to pat his head, but I soon pull away again. It's too strange to be sitting here stroking Philip's hair after the way he's treated me.

"If it hadn't been for you I would have starved to death!" he says suddenly.

"Nah," I reply. "You don't starve to death in a few days. That takes way longer."

"But still!" he says. "I would have died of thirst or hypothermia, or I would have passed out from hunger and been mawled by a bear."

"Nah," I repeat. I don't really know what to say. Plus his last comment has made me think.

"Do you really think there are bears around here?" I ask. This is a new danger that I haven't thought of at all. Even though I'm jittery from the astounding fact that Philip is sitting here in front of me crying and begging for my forgiveness, I can't stop a picture of an enormous angry bear from sneaking into my mind.

"Yeah, absolutely. Of course there are," he says, wiping his eyes with his grimy hands, leaving gray smudges on his face. "Don't you think so?"

"I have no clue," I say. "There aren't that many bears left in this area, are there?"

"No, but if there are any, they're probably around here somewhere. This forest is definitely big enough for bears," he says miserably.

At that moment I remember something. I must have

heard about it on TV. Wolves. The memory is vague, but I've definitely heard something about wolves in this area.

"Wolves," I say pitifully. "Aren't there wolves in this region?"

Philip ponders this so intensely I can almost hear his brain cells working.

"Yeah, I think you might be right. I think I've heard something about that. Or maybe we learned it at school."

"We should have paid better attention in that class," I try to joke. But Philip is not in a joking mood.

He answers in a gloomy tone, "Yeah, I guess we should have."

Involuntarily we creep closer to the safe, sunny wall and start to look around apprehensively, our eyes sweeping the edges of the darkening woods. Of course, they look the same as they always have, but right now they seem menacing. As if at any second a wolf or a bear could come charging out and go right for our throats.

"I've always heard that wolves are scared of humans," I say.

"*Heard*, yeah, exactly," says Philip ominously. "But you've never bumped into a wolf, so do you actually *know* that?"

And of course I haven't, so I keep scanning the forest's edge.

After a while we can't avoid getting up any longer. We can't spend our whole day watching for wolves. Philip goes down to the lake to dig up more reed roots, and I start cutting notches into as many birches as we have containers for. We've decided to use the plates, too, and the little pot that holds the cutlery. After that we start collecting wood. We need a big pile, so we're forced to leave the clearing and go into the woods to find more.

The forest seems much denser, darker and more inhospitable than before, so we stay very close to each other. I hear wolves everywhere, even though the only sounds are the birds singing their heads off in the trees. Just when I've started to calm down a bit I hear a massive crack. I drop all the wood I've collected and just stand where I am, screaming. Philip, on the other hand, clutches his wood as if his life depends on it. He stares, terrified, in the direction of the noise. Something big and dark is standing back among the trees. But slowly, it moves away. I stop screaming and try to pull myself together.

Philip looks calm again.

"Moose," he says.

"Yeah," I say, embarrassed that I screamed like that.

Then he laughs, a big, relieved laugh.

"I thought I was going to wet myself," he says. "Not that I was scared or anything..." he adds quickly, but then he changes his mind. "What am I talking about? Of course I was scared. Totally petrified! I guess there's no point in faking it anymore, huh?"

I pick my wood back up from the ground, and we

head back to the house to unload what we've gathered so far. The whole way back I reflect on that last thing he said. I guess there's no point in faking it anymore. I'm having a hard time absorbing what's happening with Philip. I'm so used to him treating me like an enemy that I don't quite know how to act now that he seems to think I'm his buddy. I know exactly what to do when I'm Philip's enemy: shut my mouth. But how do I act when I'm his friend? Of course I'm not a real friend, more like a stand-in friend, good enough out here in the wild when no one's watching. But still. It feels just as weird as the real thing. How do you even talk to someone like Philip? When I don't have time to think about it, I'm fine. But now that I'm trying to think of something to say to him, I can't come up with anything.

In the end, I say, "I thought I might wash those clothes now, because it doesn't matter if they're not dry by tonight. Maybe we could wash the blankets tomorrow morning." At least if I'm scrubbing the clothes I can be alone with my thoughts and won't need to find a topic of conversation.

"It seems like we'll never get around to washing those blankets," Philip says.

"Maybe tomorrow."

"Okay. Should I cook some more reed roots?" he asks. "And can you show me those leaves you told me about, curly something?"

"Curly dock," I say, darting off to point out the plants

and show him how to recognize their long leaves by the finely rippled edges.

We work on our own for a while. I warm up some water and scrub the old clothes thoroughly but carefully. Tons of dirt comes out of them, but I don't want to scrub too hard. I'm afraid they'll rip. They seem so frail. I have to change the water several times and it turns into a long, slow job. I've carried the pot with the washing out onto the grassy slope in front of the house, and I work up a good sweat with all the scrubbing, the warm water and the sunshine. It feels good to be really warm for a change. I feel like I've been slightly cold pretty much all the time for the last few days.

Out of the corner of my eye, I see Philip walking back and forth carrying things. At about the same time as I decide the washing is done, he comes over and proudly declares, "Dinner is served."

He has spread out our jackets in the grass to sit on, and there's a cup and a plate set out for each of us. On the plates are cooked, sliced reed-roots, cooked nettles and curly dock. As a decoration, he's added a few smaller uncooked curly dock leaves.

"Nice!" I say, impressed, and Philip tries not to smile.

Chapter Ten

I LIE AWAKE LONG into the night, listening for sounds out in the dark forest. No wolves howling, no bears growling. Or whatever the bears are doing, they're not growling. Maybe they just prowl around silently.

From time to time I hear strange hoots, and I assume they're from owls or hawks out in the darkness. Now and again something rattles around in the grass near the house. It's probably just a field mouse, but I still curl up tighter under the blanket. I can't stop myself from thinking it could be a wolf.

I try to block out all the other sounds by focusing on the sound of the fire crackling in the stove, but it doesn't work. By the sound of Philip's breathing, I think he must be awake. He must know that I'm awake, but he doesn't say anything. He's probably listening for sounds, too.

Mom. Dad. Sebastian. I try to blink their image out of my mind's eye, because I don't want to think about them. It's way too painful. But they won't go away. They move around in my mind, back and forth, doing the stuff they usually do, the things I long to see them do again. Mom pours me a glass of milk, and Dad cooks up some pancakes. Sebastian teases me, holding the strawberry jam so I can't reach it. Normally I can't stand him when he goes on like that, but right now I can't think of anything more wonderful than a noisy, irritating little brother. I would even let him steal my candy if I had any. If he was here. If only he was here.

I do my best to think about other people, people who don't hurt as much. I try to imagine what the other people in the class are doing at this moment. What are Emily, Amira and Saga doing? Did they make it out of the water? They must have. They were all sitting together in the back of the boat, and the guides were there with them. And all of them had life jackets on. But what if...

I can't get away from the thought that maybe they're all dead, the entire class.

It doesn't make sense that they all died, not if you really think about it and try to explain it to yourself. But nothing is as it should be right now. So why would they be alive because they *should* be? I picture a whole row of coffins, a huge funeral, with all the crying parents and siblings. The picture doesn't exactly cheer me up.

I try thinking about the ones I don't like — Vanya, Cecilia, Dunja, Frederick, and the others who never do anything but look at me like I'm a weirdo, laugh at me or say mean things to me. This doesn't help at all. Besides, Philip is one of the worst, and in the last few days I've discovered that he's almost nice. Sometimes. When he makes the effort. If you're alone with him, lost in the wild. Not that that happens very often, but still. Whatever, he's human, even if he's a pretty weird human. Maybe Vanya, Cecilia and Dunja are actually human, too.

Thinking about the people who always tease me definitely does not help. I'm just as worried about them as I am about everybody else. I don't know how many times I've wished them dead — really, seriously wished that they'd be transformed into cold rigid corpses — and now I feel horrible because that's exactly what they might be at this very moment. Vanya's beautiful face, lifeless, her new mascara washed away by the river... the thought makes me shudder.

I actually miss them. I long for them, all of them. And Teacher, who doesn't understand a thing — I miss her, too. Where are they? Why don't they come and rescue us? Why haven't we even heard people calling our names, or the sound of choppers circling around to search for us, or barking dogs following our trail? Have they forgotten us?

They can't have forgotten us. That's impossible. I know it is. But right now it seems very possible, and the thought makes me go cold inside. Everything inside me goes calm. My stomach stops growling about how hungry it is, my skin stops telling me how freezing cold it is, and my blood seems to stop moving for a moment. They have forgotten us. Of course, they have forgotten us.

Why else would they take so long? They are probably in shock about what happened. Why would they think about us?

But Mom and Dad, they must be thinking about me. They must miss me. Maybe they haven't even found out about the accident yet. Maybe they think we're still out on a harmless class trip, sleeping safe and sound in bunk beds, eating candy and telling ghost stories all night. What day is it today? Would the class trip be over yet? How many days has it been since the bus let us off at the camp? How many days have passed since I stood there looking up at the starry night sky?

The sky above this house is even larger, even darker, and covered in even more stars, yet I've already had time to get used to it. So it must have been a while ago when I was so surprised to see all those stars as I got off the bus. I try to count the days, but it's difficult. How many days have we spent collecting wood, making SOS signals and looking for things we can eat? How many nights have I slept in these blankets with the moldy smell I hardly notice anymore?

I'm so confused, because no matter how I try to figure it out, I can only count four days, and yet it feels like an eternity. Did I count correctly? I try again and again, but come up with the same result every time. Four days. And not even four whole days. It was already afternoon when we fell in the river, so really it's just three and a half days. Maybe that's not such a long time. It might not be a very long time at all when you're searching for people who are lost, especially in a huge forest like this one. And the dogs that are following our scent must have run into problems when it rained so hard that second day. The rain pounding the ground must have completely washed our scent away. Obviously it would take a while for them to find us after that.

I try to calm myself down with that thought. That it's natural that it's taken a while for them to find us. We're in a huge forest, our scent was washed away by the rain, and the people looking for us have no idea how or where we got out of the water or which direction we walked in. I add all the facts up for myself, but it doesn't make me any less worried. The more I think about how hard it will be for them to find us, the more convinced I am that we'll be stuck here forever. That someone will discover our skeletons in this house a few hundred years from now.

Philip tosses and turns now and then, trying to roll himself tighter in the blanket. He's probably brooding over the same things. I wish I could ask him. Maybe it would help to know that he's as worried as I am. But you don't share these kinds of thoughts just like that, so I keep quiet and get up to stoke the fire instead.

I sit there in front of the stove for a while, watching the flames as they move constantly into new shapes and patterns. I put a few twigs in at a time, studying how the flames grab them hungrily, changing them to light, heat and smoke. The heat eats through the wood, leaving just a few ashes. I lean in closer, letting my face heat up, turning one cheek toward the fire and then the other, absorbing the warmth until it feels like all the cold has been pushed out of my body. Then I put in a big pile of wood and lie down again, curled up under the blanket.

Chapter Eleven

THAT NIGHT I have a dream. It's really confused and bizarre. I guess dreams are almost always confused and bizarre, but this one is different.

I'm standing in the little house, but it doesn't look like the real house. Instead it's neat and clean and smells of new wood, as if it has just been built. I am wearing the dress from the cupboard, and I know I live here.

When I look out the window I see lots of bears. They seem to have surrounded the house in a tight circle, standing paw to paw. Behind the bears, a pack of wolves prowl back and forth. Now and then all the wolves sit down together and begin to howl sorrowfully at the sky. The daylight is bright outside, and yet the sky gleams with millions of stars.

In the dream I know that the animals are hungry, that they want me to give them food. So I cook a massive pot of reed roots. It must weigh at least a ton, but I lift it as easily as if it was full of cotton balls. I carry the entire pot out onto the grassy plain in front of the house, and then tip it over so the bears and wolves can reach the food.

But it's not roots that spill out on the ground. Instead, it's cooked body parts. I see Vanya's head, Frederick's arm. I recognize his watch, still attached to his wrist. A leg with Dunja's tight jeans on tumbles out, and a wolf pulls it away and starts gnawing on it. The whole thing is so incredibly horrible, and yet it's as if I knew the whole time that I was boiling my classmates, and I continue emptying them out of the pot with a huge wooden spoon. I feel sick and want to throw up, but instead I hum a little tune, as if I was just performing an ordinary household chore.

When I turn around I see Mom and Dad and Sebastian sitting on the roof, waving at me happily. Laughing, they start singing along with me. Sebastian starts running around, and suddenly he jumps down the chimney and disappears from sight. A bright orange life jacket he's waving appears over the chimney top. Now he's singing an ABBA tune from one of Dad's old vinyls. The song is SOS.

Suddenly Philip shows up. He has a long beard and a big mustache and he says, "But my dear, I've told you not to feed the wolves."

Chapter Twelve

THE NEXT MORNING I can barely open my eyes. I feel like I haven't slept a wink. The dream lingers in my mind, along with that horrible feeling.

Philip isn't around. This is the first time he's woken up before me, so I wonder what he's doing. I listen carefully to see if I can hear him, but all I can hear are the birds singing, as usual.

Suddenly I'm scared. I stiffen with fear. What if he left? What if he decided to find his way back to the river or the camp? What if he's been eaten by the wolves or the bears? Or maybe he's fallen into the lake and drowned. I want to rush out to look for him, but I'm terrified that I'll find his half-eaten body outside the door, bloody and headless.

Finally I creep to the door and go outside. Of course, there's no half-eaten Philip there. Not even a whole Philip. He's sitting down by the lake fishing, looking as peaceful as can be. He waves at me and calls out, "You're awake already? I wanted to surprise you with fresh fish for breakfast! But I haven't caught any yet."

Why on earth has neither of us thought of our fishing lines and hooks until now? All this time they've been lying buried at the bottom of our survival boxes!

"Your fishing rod is right there," calls Philip. I find a neatly cut fishing rod leaning against the outside wall, made from a long, straight branch. I grab it with one hand and wave back at Philip with the other. Normally I don't like fish very much, and at home, it wouldn't even occur to me to have fish for breakfast, but right now it sounds like a brilliant idea. I can already hear the mouth-watering sound of fish frying in the pan.

I sit down next to Philip on the round sun-warmed boulder that sticks out into the lake. The slope down to the lake is steep, so it's a great place to fish. I want the fish so badly that I don't even mind threading the worm onto the hook. I do turn my head away quickly when I break its skin, but just for a moment.

After a while Philip says, "I had a hard time falling asleep last night. You, too, right?"

"Yeah," I say.

He says nothing more. We both know why we were having a hard time sleeping. We sit there with our fishing rods, completely still and quiet, staring at the little pieces of wood we've attached as floats. Nothing happens. They just bob up and down in the rippling water. If I wasn't so dirty and hungry and scared, if it wasn't Philip I was here with, this could be a totally normal fishing trip. If it wasn't for the thousands of little "ifs" this could be a normal

Saturday or Sunday, and we'd have brought a big picnic. For the millionth time my stomach cramps up with hunger when I think of all the yummy things Mom and Dad would unload from the picnic basket. If only this was a regular fishing trip.

I shut my eyes and try to pretend that it's Mom sitting next to me. It doesn't work very well. Philip is humming a little tune, so it's hard to forget that I'm sitting beside him, and not Mom.

When I really think about it, though, I realize that I'm not half as homesick now as I was last night. Of course I want to go home, but even so, I'm kind of enjoying it here. If I had a grocery store, a bathtub and my whole family here with me, I could even imagine staying a while. And if I could be completely sure that there were no bears or wolves. I lean back against a pine trunk and doze off for a little while, until Philip pokes my shoulder and points.

My float is moving. At first I think it's just the wind, but the next moment, the float is pulled down under the surface. With a violent yank on the fishing line, I pull in the hook. Darn! There's no fish on it, but part of the worm has been eaten, so there must be something down there. Carefully I let the line out again and the hook sinks. I sit there, waiting, almost afraid to breathe.

After what feels like an eternity, the float moves again. I wait and wait, thinking about how Mom always badgers me about patience. You have to wait until the fish has bitten properly. The waiting is almost unbearable, sitting there doing nothing while the fish is so close.

At what I hope is the exact right moment I jerk the line again, even faster and harder this time. When I start pulling in the line, I definitely feel a bit more resistance than the first time. Something shimmers in the water when the hook nears the surface, and when I pull it in further I see that it's a lake trout. It struggles, dangling from the hook, and I'm terrified that it might fall back into the water, but it doesn't. The hook has a good hold. It's a puny little trout, barely bigger than my foot, but I'm overjoyed! Philip cheers next to me, and I'm so pleased I dance a little victory dance right there on the rock.

The poor fish has gotten seriously tangled up in the wire. The hook is stuck far back in its throat, and the fish keeps opening and closing its mouth. I'll have to kill it so I can get the hook out. I close my eyes, aim for a sharp edge on the rock, and whack the trout against it. Once I dare to look again the fish has stopped thrashing around, and I can coax the hook out. I feel like a murderer, and yet, I'm proud.

Then we have a feast. We put a big load of reed roots and curly dock on to boil, and we clean the fish, probably more carefully than a little trout has ever been cleaned before. We don't want to miss out on a single particle of the meat.

We both agree that we want the fish fried and not boiled, but this turns out to be difficult since we don't have any oil or butter to fry it in. We try to avoid burning it by making sure there is always a tiny bit of water in the pan, so the fish turns out more boiled than fried. But what does it matter when the aroma that fills every corner of our little house is so delicious?

I realize I do think of it that way. Our little house. Not the old hovel or the place where we're staying for a few days so we won't freeze or starve to death. No, it's our little house. As if we live here, Philip and I. As if it was a completely normal place for two kids to live. Or as if we were an old married couple. I giggle to myself at this idea. I think about my dream, where I had the old dress on and Philip had that huge beard. I can picture it, both of us wearing those old clothes and walking around like old-fashioned farmers, speaking an odd dialect and having too many kids. I giggle even louder.

"What is it?" asks Philip.

"Nothing," I say. There's no way I'm going to tell him I was picturing us married. But I can't stop giggling.

"Hey, cut it out! What's so funny?"

"Nothing, I swear!" I say. But of course he won't believe me because I can't stop laughing.

"Come on, tell me!" he pesters.

"All right, but promise you won't take it the wrong way?"

Philips shrugs. "Yeah, sure. Okay."

A few days ago, I would never have believed him if he said that. Now I actually trust him.

"Well, I realized that I was thinking about the house as our house," I say.

"Yeah, so? It is, isn't it? What's so funny about that?"

"Well, I started picturing us in those clothes we found, living here and talking in a funny accent and having loads of kids, like in a movie about the eighteenth century."

Now Philip starts laughing, too.

"Oh, my little wifey," he says, putting on a country accent. "How are we going to feed all these kids? With one puny little trout?" he drawls, raising his shoulders and smiling so it looks like he's toothless. We burst into a fit of laughter. We laugh and laugh until our stomachs are sore. We laugh so hard that we almost forget about our precious fish, which is almost burnt to the pan when we get back to it.

Chapter Thirteen

W<small>E HEAR THE STRANGE</small> sound later, when we're scarfing down our lavish meal. We've just licked the last of the fish from our fingers and divided the last root into two when we both stiffen, listening intently. Then we drop everything and run out of the house.

It's a hammering, flapping sound. Soon it's deafening.

We stare up at the sky and wave our arms with everything we've got.

Because it's the helicopter. The helicopter has finally come. I thought it never would.

"We're here!" Philip screams at the top of his lungs, even though there's no way that the people in the chopper can hear him. I don't scream but I do run around like a mad woman, waving and jumping up and down so they will see us.

The helicopter circles a few times around the house and the lake and the clearing, and I'm terrified that they haven't seen us and are turning away. But then it starts to descend slowly. The propeller whips the air around with such force that it's like being in the eye of the storm. My hair feels like it might be torn out of my head, and the grass looks like it's about to come loose from the ground. It sounds like a monster howling, even with my hands over my ears.

At last, the helicopter lands and the propeller blades go still. For a moment it feels like someone has turned off all the sound on earth, it's so quiet. The cabin door opens and a man gets out and runs over to us. He's wearing orange coveralls with a red cross on the back. I've never seen him before.

"Amanda and Philip?" he calls out, before he's even reached us.

We just nod fiercely. We're so astounded we can't say a word. Despite the fact that we've been waiting for exactly this, for someone to find us and bring us to safety, it feels so strange now that it's really happening. It feels like a movie.

"Are you okay?" the man asks, and starts looking at us to detect injuries.

We nod again.

"Have you had food and water?" the man asks.

We continue to nod. Our heads bob up and down ridiculously, like puppets.

"Any other problems? Neither of you are in any pain?"

Our heads stop nodding and start moving from side to side instead. It feels so silly, we start giggling.

The man looks at us incredulously, as if he's worried that we've lost our minds out here in the woods. I guess he doesn't think it's funny.

Another man jumps out of the helicopter, walks down to the lake, and starts kicking away the rocks from our SOS sign. At first I want to run over and tell him to stop. The sign took us almost a whole day to build, and my arms are still sore from all the work. Then I realize that it's a security measure, so no one else will think that there are people here who need help. But I can't help looking at him kind of bitterly.

"Right, then. Time to go back. There are a lot of people who are desperate to see you, and I'm guessing that there are some people you guys are desperate to see, too," says the first man, nudging us in front of him toward the helicopter.

"No, wait, I have to…" I say, but I can't think of what it is I have to do.

"…grab…" I say vaguely, and I run back toward the house. There's nothing there that I want to grab, really. I'm wearing all my clothes, and we didn't bring anything else with us. But I can't just leave this place without saying goodbye. So I go inside and stand in the middle of the room and look around. The fire has been out for a while, and our plates are still on the floor where we left them at lunch. Somehow it already looks abandoned again.

"Bye," I say. "Thanks for letting us live here."

I walk up and brush my hand against the cupboard door, touch the mangy old cot and the blankets on the floor. I pick up the plates, the pot and the pan from the floor and put them back in the cupboard. There's some food left on them, but it can't be helped. Next I pull the middle drawer open and touch the clean clothes in there. I lift up both the dresses, and think about bringing them back as souvenirs, but when I go to walk out with them over my arm, it doesn't feel right. It would be like stealing. Even though no one owns these old rags anymore I can't bring them with me. They're part of this house. They should stay here. They won't fit in with my green chest or my closet at home. They should stay here in their drawer. So I turn to leave.

"Goodbye!" I say again with a small wave, turning in the doorway. I rush out to the helicopter, and Philip stretches out a hand to hoist me up.

"What did you go back for?" he asks.

"Nothing," I say.

He looks at me quizzically, but I say nothing more. Instead I look out the window so he won't see the tears in my eyes. I've longed so much to get out of here, and now I'm strangely sad to leave our house. It's crazy.

I'd like to tell the strange men that I'm not ready to leave yet. I'm not done here, there are things I haven't had time to finish. Like the blankets I meant to wash, and my plan for fixing the leaky roof with birch bark. Last night it felt like we had been here forever, and now it feels like we only just arrived. We barely had time for anything. But they wouldn't listen to me if I asked to stay. They might even think I was traumatized and make me see a counselor. I couldn't deal with someone picking apart my memories of this place. So I sit still and keep quiet.

When the helicopter lifts, it gives me a dizzy, shaky feeling, very different from an airplane.

"Oops," Philip says suddenly. "We forgot the life jackets."

I see the two shining orange spots at the top of the old apple tree and around the birch.

"Oops," I repeat, and then we laugh again, thinking about what people will think when they find those life jackets. If anyone finds them at all.

I catch myself wondering if this is the last time Philip and I will laugh together. About something that's ours, something that's funny but only we understand why. Almost the way friends laugh together.

Because Philip and I aren't meant to laugh together. Especially not the way friends do. We belong to two different parts of the class, the school, even the world. We've just ended up in the same house for a few days, laughing at things together because there was no one else there.

Now we're on our way back to the real world.

The man in the coveralls asks us more questions. He looks in our eyes and mouths, and listens to our heartbeats and our lungs with a stethoscope. He asks what we've had to eat and drink, and whether we've vomited or had diarrhea. We tell him about the nettles, the roots, the curly dock and the fish, and he just looks at us in astonishment.

Finally he says, "Well, that's fine then!"

I turn toward the window and look back to where we came from, trying to see if I can still glimpse the house. But of course it's no longer visible. I can't even see a clearing among the trees. Nowhere where there could be a house or a grassy slope or a lake. Nowhere where old apple trees could get enough light to bear fruit. I see no roof, no smoke from the chimney, just an ocean of trees. From up here, the pine trees look so close together, it's hard to imagine that there's room to walk between them. It's unreal to think that our house is down there somewhere.

I hear the emergency medical services man talking to someone about us. He has a kind of walkie-talkie, although it's not as loud as the ones in the movies. I hear him saying, "The children have been found and are unharmed."

Hearing someone talk about you on a walkie-talkie ought to be exciting, but I'm only half-listening. All of a sudden I'm so tired, and besides, it sounded strange, as if he wasn't talking about us at all. Unharmed? Why wouldn't we be unharmed? I feel like telling him that we have names, that we were doing fine on our own, but I can't find the energy. My eyelids are much too heavy to stay open. And it would be ungrateful to complain, of course. These men did rescue us. I remember how terrified I've been, and how much I've wanted to be rescued. But just now, it's hard to remember what exactly I was so worried about. Our house was good to us.

When we land, Teacher is there. She comes running toward the helicopter before the propeller blades have even stopped, her hair blowing around her head like seaweed in a storming sea. When Philip and I step out of the cabin she hugs us hard, really hard. I hear her sobbing, and when I manage to twist my head to the side, I see there are tears running down her cheeks.

Teacher is crying. I've never seen her cry before. I've barely even seen her angry. She's the type who always has the same steady smile, whose hair is never ruffled. Now she's almost like a regular person. All of it feels a bit scary, but it's also a relief somehow. I lean my head back against her shoulder and let her cry. I peek over at Philip and he looks back at me, smiling, rolling his eyes as if to say that Teacher's a little bit nuts.

Teacher tells us that our parents have been out in the forest with a search party, but are now on their way back since they got word that we've been found. Sebastian is also with them, she says. Then she tells us that all our other classmates made it out of the river okay. Some of them have taken part in the search for us.

"Everyone has been so worried about you!" she says,

but I don't buy that for a second. Vanya, Cecilia, the others — I wonder if they've even noticed that I was gone. Maybe Emily and Amira, but I'm not sure about them either.

When I think about the class it's as if nothing has happened. As if we never fell in the river or lived in an abandoned house or went hungry together, Philip and I. Because I'm sure everything is going to be just like it always was.

Soon Philip will have forgotten everything and he'll start to tease me again. Things will return to normal in the classroom, the cafeteria, the schoolyard. Vanya will stare at my clothes and ask why I'm such a loser that I can't even get a decent pair of jeans. Emily will put up with me sometimes because she can't deal with being mean, and I'll keep pretending I'm her sort-of friend. Whatever I do will still be the wrong thing, since pretty much everyone has decided that everything about me is always just wrong. Even the class being split in two for seventh grade won't help. At least some of the people who have made up their minds about who I am will end up in my class.

Teacher stops crying after a while and lets us out of her strong hug. She puts one hand on my head and the other on Philip's and looks at us, studying our faces close-ly, as if she's forgotten what we look like.

"Are you all right? How have you managed? How has everything been?"

Then Philip says it, the extraordinary thing.

"We've been good. Amanda is great to have around, just great."

I stare at him, and he laughs. It's friendly laughter. He's not kidding.

That's the first time anyone in my class has ever said that about me.

I'm great to have around.